Switched
AT
Marriage

AVERY CHANDLER

Published by Avery Chandler
www.averychandler.com

ISBN: 978-1-7350848-2-4

Cover by Frauke Spanuth/Croco Designs
Interior formatting by Author E.M.S.

Published in the United States of America.

CHAPTER ONE

I'm pregnant. And the baby isn't yours.

Prince Amadio of Lohenberg stared at the horizon from the balcony of his bedroom, the numbness sinking deeper inside him. Any other man would have been furious, raging at his fiancée for her infidelity. As for himself, he felt only emptiness and the familiar solitude closing in.

Camille had left him that fateful voice mail, shattering their engagement and telling him that she'd gone to Italy. She'd begged him not to tell her father why.

How had this happened? He dug his fingers into the balustrade, gathering command of his emotions and transforming them into rigid control. As the heir to the Lohenberg throne, he had to maintain a calm demeanor at all times. He couldn't afford to make a rash decision or allow his own feelings to rise to the surface—not when this arranged marriage had meant a truce between his country and the neighboring kingdom of Badenstein, a means of ending the uprisings along the border checkpoints.

1

Her betrayal had cut deeply, making him wonder what he'd done wrong. He'd tried to be kind to Camille, even knowing that he wasn't her choice of husband. Truthfully, the marriage had been the King of Badenstein's demand, trying to control his daughter by forcing her into a union she hadn't wanted. Amadio had been prepared to make the best of it for the sake of peace. But he'd never imagined that the princess would go this far to avoid marriage.

No doubt his tiny country would make headlines because of a royal runaway bride. Camille had dragged both of them into a scandal that wasn't his. And what was he supposed to do now? He refused to play the part of the humiliated bridegroom, appearing weak in front of his people. No, he would demand that Badenstein relinquish all claims to the disputed territory. Then he'd send troops to guard the borders and end the attacks once and for all.

Outside, the sunlight drifted across the country he loved with its green hills and vineyards. The silvery river was calm, unlike the storm brewing inside him. Tonight, he was hosting diplomats from countries throughout Europe. It was meant to be an engagement party, a celebration of the peace to come.

He couldn't possibly attend and pretend that all was well—and yet, he could hardly cancel it at such a late time. It would be a serious breach of etiquette to deny the guests dinner. Many of them were staying at the palace, and explanations were unavoidable. But how could he admit that his bride had run away?

His mobile phone rang, and Amadio stared at Camille's number, letting it ring several times until he

2

finally let it go to voice mail. Right now, he didn't want to hear explanations about her behavior or reasons why she'd wanted someone else.

She had left him with a hell of a mess. As far as he knew, she hadn't told anyone else what had happened. Amadio was the only one who knew that there wouldn't be a wedding. A headache throbbed at his temples as he tried to think of what to do. Now, he had to find a way of keeping the media under control.

Behind him, the door opened, and he turned to see his Lord Chamberlain. "Your Highness." Johann Sichermann bowed low. "The necklace intended for your bride will be delivered to you later today. I inspected it earlier, and it's exquisite. I believe the princess will be quite pleased."

"I couldn't care less about a damned necklace," Amadio muttered. The only thing on his mind right now was how to break the news. But he trusted Sichermann above everyone else, and he needed advice. "There won't be a wedding. Camille called it off last night."

The Lord Chamberlain blanched. "I am so sorry to hear this, Your Highness. Is there…anything I can do?"

"Not unless you can find another princess from Badenstein for me to marry," he remarked drily. "There will be diplomats and dignitaries at the engagement party tonight. See to it that they enjoy their dinner and entertainment. I won't be attending."

The thought of their pity ground against his pride. Right now, his head was throbbing, and he had no desire to see anyone. It sounded quite appealing to spend the night with a bottle of whiskey and drink himself into oblivion.

The Lord Chamberlain turned thoughtful. "Forgive me, Your Highness. But there was…something unexpected that I encountered this morning. In regard to the necklace, I mean. Something that may be of use to you. Or in this case, *someone*."

"Just send it back," he ordered. He had no need of a diamond necklace anymore. "And tell King Heinrich that I want to meet with him first thing in the morning." Now that Camille had severed their arrangement, he intended to force the sovereign's hand and demand peace without a formal alliance.

"Of course, Your Highness." The Lord Chamberlain cleared his throat. "But, as I was saying, you really ought to meet with the jeweler's granddaughter. When she arrived in Lohenberg this morning at the airport, she caused quite a stir."

"What do you mean?" He had little patience for this.

"She looks exactly like Princess Camille. I mistakenly believed that she *was* the princess when I first saw her. You can only imagine how the hotel staff reacted."

A stillness slid over his mood, for he was beginning to see what the Lord Chamberlain was implying. "They could not tell the difference?"

Johann shook his head. "No, Your Highness. They were convinced she *was* the Princess of Badenstein." He winced. "Apparently she has been living in the United States all her life."

"Send her to me in a private audience," he ordered. "Let her believe it's about the necklace. And try not to let anyone else see her." Although the woman's appearance could be a strange coincidence, he needed to judge it for himself. If she looked similar enough to Camille, she might help to buy him more time. He could pass her off as the princess for a few days while he negotiated with King Heinrich, and that would avoid a tabloid storm—at least for now.

Sichermann bowed again. "Yes, Your Highness. But sir, may I suggest that you might reconsider attending the party tonight?"

Amadio gritted his teeth. The future of his country was hanging by a single thread, and he had no desire to socialize or drink champagne.

But he understood the need for discretion—at least until he could speak with the King of Badenstein about what they would do next.

Genna Hamilton stared at the Lohenberg palace and tried to gather the last remnants of her courage. It wasn't there. Although she was only here to deliver a necklace, she couldn't push back the nerves mingled with excitement. Earlier today, she had met the Lord Chamberlain when he'd inspected the necklace. Then he'd called the hotel an hour ago, asking her to bring the jewels to the palace.

Truthfully, she'd been shocked by the invitation. She'd never expected the opportunity to visit the home of the royal family. The Lord Chamberlain had sent a private car for her, and as Genna drew closer to the palace, she drank in the scenery. Brick walls surrounding the gray stone palace stretched high, while an intricate wrought iron gate stretched across the road. Around the castle, she spied several towers with copper rooftops weathered green. Ivy stretched over the surface of one tower, and she took a moment to savor the beauty. But when the black sedan pulled to a stop in front of the doors, her stomach gave a lurch of uncertainty.

She had been summoned by the Prince of Lohenberg. A prince. Her heart was pounding, and she wondered again why her grandfather had sent her to deliver the necklace, instead of coming here himself. Whenever her grandfather had spoken of Lohenberg, there'd been a wistfulness in his tone, but also the sense that he would never go back. Yet, he'd asked her to come in his place.

Genna had brought the bridal gift with her—a diamond necklace that was worth millions. A security guard sat beside her in the sedan, and the jewels were safely contained within a locked briefcase handcuffed to his wrist. She possessed the only key.

The driver opened the door, and she stepped outside into the sunlight, her heels wobbling against the gravel. Before she could take another step, she spied a door opening from the lower level. The Lord Chamberlain approached, dressed in an impeccable suit. Johann Sichermann was his name, she recalled.

"Miss Hamilton, it's good to see you again." His English had a trace of an accent, and he smiled. "If you'll just follow me." He didn't wait for an answer but led her toward the same doorway off to the side. A servant's entrance, she realized. Which made sense. She wasn't a guest here, really—only a delivery girl.

Even so, she was memorizing every inch of the gorgeous castle. How many rooms did it have? Fifty? One hundred? She hoped she would have the chance to see at least a few of the rooms before she returned to her hotel. Especially the library. She imagined a sliding ladder that stretched to the top of the bookshelves.

Mr. Sichermann led her inside and toward a narrow marble staircase. Genna glimpsed large oil portraits hanging on the walls as she rounded one staircase and climbed another, with the security guard following behind them. When they reached the landing of the third floor, Mr. Sichermann saw her lingering gaze and remarked, "That is Prince Michael and his English bride, Princess Hannah. They ruled over Lohenberg for nearly fifty years." In the oil painting, the royal couple were seated beside one another, the prince gazing into his wife's eyes.

"They look very much in love," Genna said.

"They were." Johann cleared his throat. "But unfortunately, most royal marriages are alliances not based on personal feelings."

She understood the unspoken message about Prince Amadio's wedding and offered, "Sometimes love can come later."

The expression on his face was bemused, as if he didn't really believe that. "Sometimes." He paused a moment and said, "His Royal Highness, Prince Amadio, has asked to see you regarding a personal matter."

Was it possible for her heart to pound any faster? Genna tried to behave as if it didn't matter—as if she met princes all the time. "Of course. He will want to see the necklace."

"After he has spoken with you," he corrected. To the security guard, he said, "You will wait outside until the prince sends for you."

Genna wasn't certain what to think about that, but there was no reason to argue since she had the briefcase key. "All right."

Mr. Sichermann continued down the hall until he reached a room with double doors. Three chairs were outside, and he motioned for the security guard to take a seat. Then he knocked at the door.

Genna heard a man's voice commanding them to enter, and her anxiety ratcheted up a notch. Was this a throne room of sorts? She imagined a large wooden chair and wondered if anyone else would be there. His fiancée, the Princess of Badenstein, perhaps?

She had no more time to wonder before Mr. Sichermann opened the doors and said, "Please go inside."

Genna hesitated but obeyed, expecting the older man to join her. Instead, she was startled when he closed the doors behind her, leaving her alone with Prince Amadio.

Oh my, was all she could think when she saw him for the first time. Although he was seated behind a large wooden desk, she could tell that the prince was quite tall. He wore a charcoal gray suit, and his black hair was combed back. His sun-warmed skin was a stark contrast against the white color of his shirt, and the top two buttons were open. He was a walking men's cologne advertisement.

A flush slid over her cheeks, for she hardly knew what she was supposed to do. Curtsy? Shake his hand? What should she say?

At last, she decided to introduce herself. "I'm Genna Hamilton." She stepped closer and offered her hand, but he remained seated at the desk and didn't take it. Awkwardly, she let her hand fall to her side.

"The jeweler's granddaughter," he said, and she nodded.

Even though he was behind a desk, power radiated from his demeanor. The prince stared at her as though he couldn't quite decide whether to toss her out or allow her to stay. His gaze remained fixed upon her face. Behind his blue eyes, she saw the flare of a response she didn't understand. Had she done something wrong?

"Would you like to see the necklace for the princess?" she ventured. "My security guard is holding it right outside. I'd be happy to answer any questions about it if you'd like."

His expression sharpened, and behind those ice-blue eyes, she sensed that there was something he wanted from her.

This commission was critical, one she and her grandfather couldn't afford to lose. Not only because of the ten million dollars, but also because the princess would be photographed in the necklace. It was a once-in-a-lifetime chance to bring Seraphina Jewels into the international spotlight.

Her grandfather needed her help, and she intended to do everything possible to ensure that the Prince of Lohenberg was pleased with the necklace.

"Are you aware of your resemblance to Princess Camille?"

Genna almost flinched at the question. "Um…I don't really know." She didn't want to admit that she'd paid little attention to the wedding, much less the bride. She'd barely heard of Badenstein until a few months ago, since it was such a small country near Germany. She was embarrassed that she'd never bothered to look at photos of the prince and princess online.

And it wasn't exactly polite to tell a prince that she'd paid no attention to his wedding—her entire focus had been upon designing the necklace.

But it wasn't entirely her fault that she'd ignored the outside world. Her grandfather had led a simple life in upstate New York, refusing to allow technology into his home. He had no computer, no internet, and it was a wonder that he'd permitted electricity. Her only access to the web had been at school. Even the Seraphina website was run by a business partner, and it redirected buyers to their store in New York City. Genna had never been to the city, for that was her grandfather's domain. She was content to work in her studio at home.

Years ago, her friends had teased her about Grandfather's hermit ways, but the truth, they'd enjoyed coming over to his house. They'd played board games, baked cupcakes, and there was a sense of stepping back in time. And really, she didn't think it mattered. Sometimes it was nice to wash the dishes by hand and just talk. Maybe that made her old-fashioned, but she didn't care. She designed jewelry, so why did it matter if she isolated herself from the world?

The prince stood from his desk and crossed to stand in front of her. His gaze was penetrating, as if he were pushing back every layer to find the woman beneath. "I need someone to stand in for the princess tonight. A great many dignitaries have traveled to celebrate my engagement, and Camille cannot attend the party."

She blinked at that. "I'm sorry, what?" Surely, she hadn't heard him right. Someone to stand in for the princess?

His presence unnerved her, for he was fixated upon

her appearance. "You're going to pretend to be Camille tonight."

Well, that was blunt. And he hadn't exactly asked— he'd commanded her.

"No," she blurted out. "I can't do that." She knew nothing about how a princess was supposed to behave in public. And why would he ask her, a perfect stranger, to fill such an important role? It was impossible.

"Why don't you just tell everyone she's not feeling well?" she suggested. "You can attend, and it won't matter if Princess Camille isn't there."

"I have my reasons," he said. "All you have to do is take her place. It's temporary." The hard expression on his face warned her that there was more to this than he was telling her. He wanted the outside world to believe that everything was normal. Why else would he go through such a ruse?

"Johann will show you everything you need to know. Just wear a gown, smile, and don't speak to anyone. If you remain by my side, no one will know the difference."

He was insane if he thought she could pull this off. There was no way it would work. "Absolutely not. I'm not going to pretend to be a princess. This is your engagement party, not Halloween." The very idea was horrifying. There was no reason why he should go through with such an elaborate façade.

Unless…something had gone wrong. Something ominous that he didn't want anyone to know about. What if something had happened to the princess?

"Has she gone missing?" Genna ventured. "Was she kidnapped?"

Prince Amadio's gaze had gone cold, and he ignored her question. "I don't want to alert the media. It's best if we go on as if all is well."

Then she was right. He wanted her to stand in, so that no one would know Camille was gone. If they were quietly looking for the princess, it might be safer if the outside world believed she was still here.

Genna had vaguely heard that there had been fighting along the borders between Badenstein and Lohenberg. And if the princess had been kidnapped, it could mean an outbreak of war. "Then she's...missing?"

Another nod, but she sensed that there was something else he wasn't telling her. "I'm so sorry," Genna said quietly. "You must be so afraid for her. I hope she's found quickly."

His gaze swept over her, and he said, "There's not much time before the party this evening. You will have to look exactly like Camille. Johann will see to it that you have a stylist to help you with your hair and so forth."

"But—"

"When you attend the party tonight, we will claim that you're recovering from losing your voice. You will wear the necklace." He eyed her more intently, and she felt the scrutiny of his gaze. "It's a business opportunity for you."

She knew he was referring to the necklace, but this kind of opportunity wasn't what she'd been hoping for. The thought of being the center of attention terrified her. There were a hundred ways to screw it up.

"This isn't a good idea," she insisted. "I don't know anything about behaving like a princess. I still think you should tell everyone she's sick. It would be easier." She shook her head. "I'm sorry, but I can't do it."

The coldness on his face grew more calculating. "Then I'll send the necklace back with you."

The air seemed to leave her lungs. Although Prince Amadio had already paid half the commission, the majority of the money had paid for the diamonds. They needed this sale to keep the company afloat. But worse, if the prince refused the necklace, the outside world would believe that Seraphina jewels were not good enough. It could cause irreparable damage to her grandfather's business.

It was a power play—she could see it in his eyes. Prince Amadio was accustomed to getting what he wanted. And for some reason, he wanted her to make everyone believe that his engagement would continue as planned.

"What happened to the princess?" she asked quietly.

He ignored her question. "If you do as I ask, everyone will know that the necklace was made by Seraphina. You will be photographed in the jewels. That will be enough publicity in return for your cooperation."

His voice was resonant, but she didn't miss the subtle threat. It irritated her that he was trying to intimidate her for his own gain. Unfortunately, she didn't see a choice. And though she was inwardly quaking, she lifted her chin and demanded, "Wire the remainder of the money to my grandfather, and I'll do it. But I'll only switch places with her for tonight."

He drew closer and she felt eclipsed by his broad frame. She inhaled the clean scent of his aftershave, and she suddenly wondered what it would be like to kiss such a man. His presence emanated power and domination.

He was accustomed to getting whatever he wanted, and she wasn't used to male attention. When he put his hands on her shoulders, her thoughts scattered like marbles rolling across the floor.

"One week," he countered. "You will pretend to be the princess, and if no one learns the truth about your identity, I'll wire the remainder of the payment." He reached out to cup her nape. The heat of his touch made goosebumps break out over her skin. She imagined him pulling her closer, claiming her mouth with his. The vision was electric, though she knew it was only a royal fantasy.

"In addition, if you play the role well enough, I will reward you with another million dollars for your trouble."

Well enough? What did he mean by that? Color flooded her face, and she shook her head. "I won't sleep with you. I'm not that kind of woman."

There was a faint softening at his eyes. "That wasn't what I was asking. But you may need to pretend... affection you don't feel."

In other words, she might have to kiss him in public or hold his hand. It seemed almost incongruous that such a gorgeous man would pay her to do this. Just because she looked similar to a princess.

"What is your decision?" he demanded.

Six million dollars. For one week of pretense. It felt as if the air had been sucked out of her lungs, and Genna sat down. It was a dangerous game he was playing, and she didn't entirely understand why he didn't just tell the world that his princess was missing. She wanted to ask again, but something made her hold back.

"I will try it for tonight," she answered. "And I will decide afterwards, if I can handle it for the rest of the week."

Though he ought to be relieved that Genna was willing to stand in for his bride, Amadio felt a sense of unrest instead. Common sense warned that he ought to reveal Camille's disappearance and her decision to call off the engagement. But he didn't want any more negative press toward Lohenberg. His country was already viewed as the aggressor in the border disputes, and this marriage was meant to be a distraction and a means of peace. Without a royal wedding to bring Lohenberg into a more positive light, he had to find another way of managing his country's image. If that involved a night of deception, so be it.

"Do you…want to see the necklace now?" Miss Hamilton asked.

He shrugged. Truthfully, he hardly cared what it looked like. The jewelry mattered to her, but he would only pay the remainder of the commission if she was successful in her role-playing.

She went to the door and opened it, instructing her guard to bring the jewels inside. Then she opened the blue velvet case and revealed the necklace. Amadio hardly paid any attention to her description of the flawless diamonds, but instead, he took a moment to discreetly study her. She wore a blue wrap dress around her slim body, and it revealed soft curves and long legs. Her blond hair was shorter than Camille's, but that could be disguised with the right styling. Her eyes were the same, and she had the identical patrician nose. But unlike Camille, Genna had a stubborn streak. Most people didn't even attempt to bargain with him because they knew they would lose. And yet, she had made demands of her own.

Her determination was either going to be a big problem or it would prove that she had the courage to handle the immense pressure.

He lifted his gaze to hers and studied her features more closely. There was something refreshingly bold about this woman, as if she cared nothing about what anyone else thought. And he didn't know what sort of behavior to expect from her.

"Put on the necklace," he commanded. "I want to see what it looks like on you."

She did, and he studied the tiered jewels hanging around her neck, the large teardrop diamond nestled above her breasts. He couldn't remember how many carats she'd said it was, but the diamond was larger than his thumb. In the sunlight, the jewels sparkled against her skin.

Her resemblance to Camille made it hard to look at her. It was as if another version of his bride had stepped into this room. He wondered if she was a bastard daughter from someone related to King Heinrich. There was no denying the possibility.

"You will need the right gown to wear this necklace," he pointed out. "Did you bring something appropriate?"

She bit her lower lip. "I suppose I'll have to go out dress shopping."

"No, the gowns will be brought to you," he said. "In Lohenberg, princesses do not go out in public to shop."

"Then it's a good thing I'm not a princess," she said in a teasing voice. A faint smile caught her lips, and he realized that this deception might be dangerous. Trusting her was a risk he shouldn't take.

"Tell Johann your size, and he will have several selections delivered to your room. You have six hours to prepare yourself for the party tonight. I need you to look *exactly* like Camille. You cannot make a single mistake."

"I'm aware of that."

He reached out to help Genna remove the diamonds, and her fingers brushed against his. They were cold, as if he'd made her nervous. The clasp was complicated, but he unfastened it slowly, his thumbs resting against the line of her neck.

Camille had once accused him of being a frigid man with no passion at all. It was true. He'd learned the hard way, years ago, never to let himself fall in love. He'd been young and stupid, infatuated with a beautiful debutante—until his father had sent the woman away. She'd sold her story to a tabloid, filling the pages with stories that embarrassed him even now. The king had warned him never again to lower his guard. "Don't ever be foolish enough to think that a woman loves you. She loves your title and your money. But never you."

Over the years, his father had been proven right, time and again. By the time he'd become engaged to Camille, Amadio had learned his lesson well. He'd never felt much of anything for her, and now, her cheating only infuriated him.

A part of him wanted to prove that he *could* be seductive to a woman, drawing her under his spell and into his bed. And for that reason, his hands lingered upon Genna's neck. She could have pulled away, but instead, he saw goosebumps rise up on her skin. When he pulled the diamonds away, she turned to face him.

There was interest in her eyes and a faint blush on her cheeks. When she stood up from the chair, she had to tilt her head back to meet his gaze. Amadio took another step closer, but Genna held her ground. Fear loomed behind her green eyes, but her soft lips enticed him. He imagined sliding his hands into her hair, dragging her down for a kiss.

She's not Camille. He was well aware of that. But there was more about this woman that he didn't know. And he looked forward to uncovering her secrets.

"Do you like it?" she asked, her voice breaking.

"Yes." His voice went husky as he imagined this woman wearing nothing but the necklace.

"Good." She swallowed hard. "I guess I'll need to start getting ready for tonight. What do you want me to know about the guests?"

"Nothing at all. As I said before, I want you to remain silent and walk with me. Smile. Perhaps dance."

"I'm guessing you mean slow dancing, right?"

"Obviously." But he saw the amusement in her eyes. She bit her lip, as if trying to imagine a royal dance party.

Genna managed to regain her composure and turned serious again. "Are you certain you don't want to just tell everyone the truth? It might help you find her faster."

He thought about revealing it to her but decided against it. Instead, he shook his head. "Go with Johann, and he will find a stylist to help you prepare. Whatever you do, don't speak to anyone about this." He reached for her hand, needing her to understand the precarious position he was in. He had no qualms about being ruthless.

"Don't fail in this, Miss Hamilton. A great deal lies at stake."

CHAPTER TWO

Over the past few hours, Herr Sichermann had been like Genna's fairy godfather, finding her a dress and sending someone to make her appear exactly like Princess Camille. The stylist had pulled Genna's blond hair into a sleek, classic twist before she'd created a flawless complexion with cosmetics. Genna hardly recognized herself, but there was no doubt that she did now resemble the princess. She wore an off-the-shoulder couture red gown that probably cost thousands. Loosely draped silk clung to her shoulders before it plunged to a low neckline, revealing the diamond necklace. The stylist had also given her four-inch heels to match the gown. Genna figured if she made it through the evening without twisting an ankle, it would be a miracle.

She ought to feel amazing in this dress and the necklace she'd designed. Instead, panic welled up, and she was afraid she might start hyperventilating. She couldn't play this role. Why had she ever believed she could? She'd never been to an event like this, with so many important people and royalty. This wasn't just a dress-up game. The real princess's life was in danger. If she messed up and her deception was revealed, she might cause Camille to be hurt.

Her heart was pounding as she stared at the mirror, trying to gather her courage to call it off. It was safer for everyone.

And yet, she'd already given her consent for tonight, so now wasn't the best time to turn coward.

Genna was trying to decide what to do, when suddenly the door opened. Prince Amadio stood at the entrance, staring at her. For a moment, he appeared shocked, as if he couldn't believe what he was seeing. His expression faltered as his gaze passed over her in a silent inspection.

"Do I look like her?" she asked, feeling her cheeks flush.

He gave a single nod. And yet, behind his cool blue eyes, she sensed a sudden heat of interest. It unnerved her, for she didn't believe it was possible to measure up to the princess.

"Are you ready?" he asked.

"Not really," she whispered. Her skin had turned to ice, but she blurted out, "I shouldn't do this. It's a lie. I'm going to make mistakes, and they'll know I'm a fraud."

He closed the door behind him and stood a short distance back. "You're afraid."

"Of course, I'm afraid. I don't know what I'm doing." She stood up from the dressing table and nearly stumbled in the heels. "See, I don't even know how to walk."

"You'll manage for six million dollars," he remarked.

His words were an invisible blow to her feelings,

and she had to say something. "That's not why I did this. It's not about the money." *Well, not exactly.* "I did it to help your bride if she's in danger. But that doesn't mean it was the right choice." She held on to the back of the chair, steadying her feet. "If you want me to back out, just say the word."

For a long moment, he studied her, remaining silent. His expression was like a stone wall, revealing nothing. She couldn't guess his thoughts, but it didn't matter.

"What is it you're afraid of?" he continued.

She thought about it, considering the truth. "I've never been the center of attention before. I don't want everyone looking at me or judging me by my appearance," she added. "I won't measure up."

He took a step closer, and his presence seemed to eclipse the space. She could smell the clean scent of him, and she was drawn to his broad shoulders and height. He looked like a man who would never let any harm come to his family. And something about his overbearing nature caught her curiosity.

"Look at me, Miss Hamilton," he said in a low voice.

"Genna," she corrected. But she obeyed and was caught up in his blue eyes. For a moment, she saw a glimpse of the man behind the prince—someone who understood what it was like to be in this position, where everyone would stare. He took her hands and tucked one into his arm.

"You won't embarrass yourself. And you won't make a mistake. I won't allow it."

"And what if I do?" her voice came out in a slight whisper. "If they discover who I really am, would someone hurt your bride?"

"No," he said quietly. "But I might have you thrown into the dungeons."

His sudden humor surprised her, and she quipped, "Well, then. There's motivation for you."

He did smile then, and the transformation stole her breath. Prince Amadio was a gorgeous man, but within seconds, his expression shifted back to business. It was as if the invisible wall had returned.

"I—I don't have an engagement ring," she said. "They'll know."

"We'll tell them it's being resized," he said smoothly. He offered his arm, and she took it, feeling well out of her element. "It's going to be all right, Miss Hamilton."

Genna didn't know what she was walking into or what might happen, but somehow, she believed that he wasn't going to let her embarrass herself. She took a deep breath and steeled herself. "I'll do my best."

He rested his hand on top of hers in silent reassurance, and her heart began to beat even faster.

Amadio kept Genna's hand in his as he mingled among the guests. Her fingers were freezing, but he had to admit, she was quite the actress. Many times, she looked at him with a warm smile, and it appeared so genuine, he wanted to believe it was real. She looked so much like Camille, and yet there was no trace of the usual sadness in his fiancée's eyes.

It was quite possible that Genna would cause a stir among the guests, though not for the reasons she might think. Camille rarely stood at his side. Instead,

23

she tended to find a friend and remain in the shadows. In contrast, Genna was gripping his hand as if she drew strength from him. And Amadio felt a protective instinct to shield her from those who could possibly discover the truth.

She smiled at the guests again, and he murmured under his breath, "You're doing quite well."

"My feet went numb an hour ago from these heels," she whispered back. "I'm dying a slow death."

"Just a few more hours." He led her towards a table of hors d'oeuvres, walking slowly so she would not stumble in the heels.

"Easy for you to say," she mumbled. "You're not wearing torture devices." When they reached the food, he started to give her a plate, but she said, "No, you choose food for both of us. I'll get us each a glass of champagne."

Before he could argue, she stepped towards a servant and took two glasses. And then, the Danish ambassador arrived to speak with her. This could be a disaster—especially since the ambassador was a distant cousin of Camille's. Amadio set down the plate and crossed to her side, only to hear the ambassador speaking to her in his own language. Genna's expression was warm and friendly, though she did not speak.

"Ambassador, it's good to see you." Amadio addressed him in his native tongue. "Forgive the princess, but she has had a sore throat and has lost her voice."

The older man relaxed. "I am sorry to hear it. I hope you feel better soon, Princess Camille."

She nodded to the man and let Amadio lead her back

to the table. He offered her the plate, and she took a piece of cheese. "Don't let yourself be alone with any of the guests," he warned. "It's not safe."

Genna ventured an apologetic smile. "I'm sorry. He was just suddenly there before I could do anything."

Likely because they had been avoiding everyone. "I suppose we should greet some of the guests," he acceded. "I'll do the talking, and you just smile. Do *not* speak."

"Well, if you want, I could—"

"Absolutely not." He didn't want her accidentally giving her identity away. "For now, just pretend to be someone you're not."

"Quiet and obedient, you mean?"

He didn't miss her sarcasm. "It's for a week. You'll live."

"For one night," she corrected. "If these heels don't kill me first." Her face turned pained. "I may never walk again after these blisters." But she joined him as he went to speak to several foreign dignitaries. This was about keeping up appearances, and he switched into German, Italian, and French as he greeted each of them. Many of them complimented her necklace, which was what she'd wanted. Genna kept up her end of the bargain by smiling and nodding.

When they crossed the room, she whispered, "Just how many languages do you know?"

"Five fluently." He'd been forced to learn the languages of most of the neighboring countries out of necessity. It was part of being a prince—both out of respect for others and to ensure that language was never a barrier.

"I'm impressed. I had high school Spanish, and of course, my grandfather speaks—"

She never got to finish her sentence when suddenly, the violins and piano began to play. The guests turned their attention to them, and they began to applaud.

"We have to lead the first dance," the prince told her.

"Oh, no. Bad idea. I'm not good at dancing."

"Then let me lead, and just pretend you know how," he told her. He slid his hand around her waist and drew her toward the center of the dance floor. "Look into my eyes, not at your feet. Now take a step backwards and then a step to your left, and a step forward." She did, and he kept the tempo slow enough so she could follow. The instruments began to play a slow version of a popular love song, and soon other couples joined them.

Once or twice she stumbled, but he masked it by grasping her waist. "Good. You're starting to follow the pattern."

"It would be easier without these heels. My blisters have blisters by now." In spite of her pain, she did manage to smile. "You know, it might be easier if I were barefoot. Do you think anyone would notice if I kick off my shoes?"

"Yes. Don't even consider it." But the daring look in her eyes made him realize that she just might do it. There was something impulsive about her, as if beneath that polished beauty lay a rebel. What surprised him more was that he was intrigued by it. He shut down the idea, for right now, he didn't need another woman disrupting his life. He needed to somehow get through the next week.

He continued dancing with her, and she said, "Thank

you for helping me with the dance. I think I'm getting the hang of it." With another light smile, she added, "I couldn't do this without your help."

Neither could he, but he didn't admit it. She had given him the means of saving face, though he still didn't know what to do about the broken engagement. It was best to speak with King Heinrich to renegotiate their agreement before any other decisions could be made.

"You're doing well," he said to Genna. "Just a few more hours."

"Hours of torture?" she quipped. "Somehow, I thought being a princess would be more fun."

"If you stay for the week, you might find it more enjoyable." He leaned closer, his temple resting against hers. Though it was only a diversion for those watching, he noticed the way she stiffened against him—as if she didn't want him this close to her.

"Try to endure the dance a little longer," he said against her ear before he pulled back. "You won't have to dance with me again."

Her cheeks were burning, but she admitted, "It's not that." She gave an awkward smile. "It's just that…I've never slow danced before. I wasn't much for dances in high school or college."

That *did* surprise him. "No one asked you to dance?"

She grimaced. "Grandfather didn't want me to go to the dances. Sometimes I went anyway, with some of my friends, but never with a boy. And later, I was too caught up in my jewelry designing to worry about a relationship."

Her confession made him feel almost possessive, though that was ridiculous. They weren't going to spend that much time together, so it hardly mattered that he'd been her first dance partner.

But it did make his mind go down another path, wondering if any man had been her first lover. Somehow, he suspected she hadn't let anyone touch her and he was glad of it.

His hand rested at her waist against the thin silk until it felt as if his bare palm were touching her skin. As he led her in a slow circle, his senses were heightened. He could smell the light perfume of her shampoo and a hint of lotion upon that skin. It bothered him, for he had never been this aware of Camille. Their dancing had been polished...and yet empty. The princess had tolerated his arms around her, but never had she rested her chin against his shoulder the way Genna did just now.

"I'm not as scared as I was before," she admitted. "Although my feet do hurt, this isn't so bad."

She sounded so innocent, almost as if she didn't mind being in his arms. He couldn't remember any time in his life when a woman had looked at him in this way or spoken so freely. They all wanted to use him in some way. But this woman was still hesitant about whether to spend the next week with him.

Suddenly, all around them, there came the distinct clinking of glasses. Amadio felt her body tense. He knew what that meant—that they should kiss. It *was* an engagement party after all.

"You don't have to," he said.

"It's all right," she answered. "It doesn't mean anything. Go ahead."

He leaned in, planning to simply brush his lips against hers. But the moment he did, her mouth parted.

She drew her arms around his neck, offering herself. And when she kissed him back, a primal hunger seemed to awaken within him. Her mouth was warm, yielding sweetly.

His heart pounded as he claimed her lips. Though he knew he needed to stop, a dormant part of him craved her affection. And then he shut it down, reminding himself that this was false—just like the other women who had pretended to care, later proving that they were only interested in becoming Princess of Lohenberg.

She doesn't want you. She only wants your six million dollars.

He pulled back, gathering command of himself until the wall of solitude was back in place. Genna's cheeks were red, and he could feel her fingers trembling.

"I've had enough of this," he said quietly. "We're done with the party."

She turned serious and nodded. "All right."

Amadio led her past the applauding guests, faking a light smile. Her kiss had shaken him, and he needed to return to reality, where his brain would remember that none of it was real.

Amadio passed by Johann and ordered him to ensure that the champagne kept flowing. He'd done his duty and attended the party, but he was finished now.

"As you wish, Your Highness." Johann bowed, and Amadio led Genna toward a side door. Before he could open it, the ambassador from Badenstein stepped forward. Amadio had never liked the man, for the ambassador reminded him of a reptile with his cold eyes and stare.

"Do you really believe anyone would think you are

our princess?" he murmured to Genna, deliberately speaking in his native tongue.

Amadio was about to interrupt, when Genna stopped and stared down at the man. In the same language, she answered, "Why wouldn't they?"

◈

Genna knew she'd taken a serious risk just now, but she couldn't just nod and smile to that awful man. From his remark, she'd guessed he was from Badenstein, but her grandfather had taught her their language ever since she was a little girl. She'd understood every word, and for some reason, his words had ignited her anger. He was trying to start a fight with the prince, and she wasn't about to let him get by with the insult.

Amadio was gripping her arm as they departed, and she knew that she'd made him furious. He said not a word but guided her down a narrow hallway and up a staircase until he opened a small sitting room. A warm fire blazed in the hearth with gas logs, and when he released her arm, she sat down on the couch and took off the heels.

"You didn't have to haul me away," she said.

Amadio's face was dark with anger. "How could you possibly know his language?"

"My grandmother was from Badenstein and my grandfather spent most of his life there, though he was born in Lohenberg," she answered. "I've known the language from the time I was little." In fact, she was pretty sure they spoke the same language in both countries, since the boundaries between the two were constantly shifting.

"That was an unnecessary risk you shouldn't have taken."

Oh, he was furious. But he had no reason to take out his anger on her.

"Maybe so, but he was acting like a jerk. I wanted to put him in his place." She reached for her foot, wincing at the blisters. It looked like one had begun bleeding.

"Were you ever planning to tell me you could speak our language?" he demanded. "Or were you going to keep that a secret?" From the tone of his voice, it was clear that he thought she'd been hiding it from him.

"Actually, I tried to tell you about it. I said that I took Spanish in high school, and I was going to tell you that Grandfather had taught me your language. But you cut me off before I could say anything."

The prince had gone ice cold again, and his features appeared to be carved from stone. Then he switched into his native language, testing her ability. "Who are you really?"

She answered him in the same dialect. "I'm Genna Hamilton, as I told you before. Nothing's changed."

But from his expression, she could tell that he didn't believe her. He probably thought she was lying about her identity. What was there to lie about? She had lived in New York all her life, and her grandfather had raised her. Her mother had died in childbirth. End of story.

The prince was staring at her as if he thought she had deliberately tried to manipulate him. Nothing could be further from the truth. Genna stood barefoot on the carpet and faced him down. "Look, if you want me to go, I'll go. I just...wanted you to pay the rest of the commission for the necklace. But if you don't want me to stay—if you're too suspicious of me or if you think I'll be a problem, I'll leave right now."

"I do think you've withheld information from me. And I want to know everything."

She crossed her arms and regarded him. "What do you want to know? That my grandfather happens to speak your language? He left Badenstein years ago and never went back. I'm sure there are many others who did the same."

"And what about your face?" he asked softly. "Surely you must believe there's a connection to Camille. How could you not?"

"Even if there was a connection somehow, my mother never lived to tell me about it. I don't know who my father was, and no one ever came looking for me. They didn't care, Your Highness. I was nothing, a nobody." She raised her chin and stared at him. "They didn't want me, and I don't want them. I've made my life in the U.S., and when this is over, I'm going home."

The prince stared at her for a long time, as if trying to decide whether to believe her. Then he crossed the room and opened another door leading to a small bathroom. He retrieved a first aid kit from beneath the sink and went to sit beside her on the couch.

"I don't tolerate lies. Not from anyone."

"I'm telling you the truth." She started to reach for the kit, but he opened it instead. Then he reached for a tube of antibiotic ointment and took her foot into his lap. When he smoothed the medicine on one of the blisters, she was startled by his touch. She almost wanted to move her foot away, but she couldn't understand what he was doing. Or why.

"I never lied to you," she said quietly. "Not once."

He said nothing but took a bit of gauze and wrapped it around her blistered heel. She was transfixed by him, so confused by the contrast of his words and his actions. For a moment, he held her foot, watching her with that shielded expression. It made her remember the kiss and how it had unraveled her good sense.

Yes, it had been for the benefit of the guests, but she'd been so overwhelmed by the heat of his mouth upon hers. She'd never been kissed like that—as if he couldn't get enough. And God help her, she wanted to experience it again. She wanted to know what it was for the rest of the world to fall away while she was caught up in his embrace.

But despite the forbidden attraction, her conscience reminded her that it wasn't right. She wasn't the prince's fiancée, and none of this was real. He belonged to another woman, and it had only been a role to play.

Don't let yourself fall for him, she warned. Though it might be a fairytale, being swept away by a handsome prince, she knew better than to believe in that.

She pulled her foot away from him and asked, "Do you want me to go or stay the rest of the week?"

"I don't know yet." He leaned closer, and those blue eyes held her captive. "I want to know the answers about you first."

"I've already told you everything I can."

"No." He cut her off, silencing her with a look. "There's far more to this. And I intend to find out what happened."

CHAPTER THREE

Amadio didn't know what to think about Genna's revelation, but he reminded himself that within a week, she'd be gone. If she did have an unknown connection to Badenstein, he wouldn't allow it to pose a threat—nor would he allow her or anyone else to use him. He had already decided to hire a discreet investigator to learn more about her family.

He'd also arranged a meeting with the King of Badenstein, and then he would decide the best means of publicly ending the engagement. The problem was that several European newspapers had published photographs of him dancing with Genna last night—and the press had been quite positive. Without even realizing it, her smile had helped ease some of the political tension.

But it had done nothing to alleviate his own frustration. No matter how he'd tried to distance himself, she had a way of pushing through the invisible boundaries. Last night, he hadn't been able to stop thinking about the kiss. It had been many years since a woman had kissed him in that way—as if she truly wanted *him* and not his title. But he knew better than to believe the feigned affection. It was part of being a prince. Women wanted the promise of a fairytale, not the man he was. It was better if he turned his attention to his country's problems and not the beautiful woman who tempted him to let down his guard.

He decided to find her and set down the rules between them. Genna needed to know his expectations, and he had to ensure that there would be nothing between them beyond their interactions this week.

Amadio finished his breakfast and went in search of her. He spoke with Johann, who told him she was enjoying her meal by the pool. She'd spent last night at the palace after they had discreetly brought her belongings from the hotel.

When he arrived outside, he saw Genna wearing a robe, sitting beside his father, the king. Amadio hurried down to the pool area, wondering if it would be a good day for his father or one where his heart problems would cause even more exhaustion. Ever since his father's illness, Amadio had taken on more of the responsibilities, but sometimes it felt like a burden.

"Good morning, Father," he said.

Stefan turned, a cynical smile on his face. "It is, isn't it?" From the look in the king's eyes, he was fully aware of what was going on. But Amadio couldn't tell whether Genna had fooled him or not. His father continued, saying, "Your bride was telling me about the party last night. I'm sorry I wasn't well enough to attend."

"I'm sorry, too," Genna answered, speaking the Lohenberg language. Her accent was flawless, and it was only if he listened carefully that Amadio could catch a slight difference. "It was very nice. There was music, and good food." The kindness on her face was genuine, but when she risked a glance at him, he sensed her discomfort.

"I imagine it was quite different from what you're used to," Stefan said to Genna. Again, his father sent a knowing look back at him. It was possible that he'd guessed the deception, though Amadio couldn't say for certain.

"I've never attended my own engagement party, if that's what you mean," Genna said smoothly.

The king laughed and remarked, "How much is he paying you?"

There was no denying the truth now. He didn't know how his father had discovered the deception, but before Amadio could intervene, Genna's anger flared. "Why would you say something like that?"

Amadio wanted to curse. He'd needed her to keep up the ruse, but it had taken less than a minute for his father to guess. This would never work.

Stefan shrugged. "Because whatever he's planning to pay affects me. It *is* our family money, after all. I may be willing to offer more if you leave our country now."

"No." Amadio cut his father off. "Stay out of this, Father."

"Oh, come now. She knows how this game is played. I suppose you offered her money to stand in for Camille, since she's gone." His father straightened in his chair.

Genna dropped all pretenses. "Prince Amadio did ask me to help him control the situation," she admitted. "But whether or not I leave is up to him. If I make a promise, I keep it."

Yet, the king appeared amused. "How long did he hire you for?"

"A week." She stared at him. "His bride is in danger, and he asked me to take her place until she's found."

Stefan began laughing. "Oh, I know exactly where Camille is. Likely staying at her villa in Italy, if I remember correctly. She's in no danger, I can assure you. Amadio wanted you here so he could call off the engagement without looking like the jilted bridegroom."

"Stay out of this," Amadio warned his father again. If it were possible to order the king to leave, he'd do so. As it was, he intended to remove Genna from his presence before Stefan interrogated her further.

But he hadn't counted on Genna's anger. "I wasn't aware that Camille left. But if that's true, I'd have thought you'd have more sympathy." She raised her chin and regarded him. "If my presence allows Prince Amadio to save face, who cares? If Camille did run off to Italy, the King of Badenstein ought to be apologizing. Amadio did nothing wrong."

She was defending him? He could hardly believe what she'd said. He reached for her hand and said, "We're leaving."

"Not yet." Genna continued. "You won't have to see me after this week, Your Majesty. But your son is doing everything he can to control the situation. With all due respect, leave him alone."

There was a hard glint in his father's eyes, as if he wanted to cut her down for what she'd said. Instead, he rose from his chair. "You won't last three days." He lifted his hand, and one of the attendants came to help him up. "You'd be wise to cut your losses and take my offer."

Then he departed with the attendant, leaning heavily on the man as he helped him up the stairs.

Amadio waited until his father had gone, using the time to calm his anger. He should have known that Stefan would come after Genna. The king had eyes and ears everywhere, and despite his failing health, he remained cognizant of every possible threat.

No one knew how much time Stefan had left. Though Amadio was prepared to be king, he was aware that his father had never had much faith in him. Stefan had done everything in his power to eradicate emotion, to ensure that Amadio ruled over Lohenberg without ever allowing his reactions to show.

Once they were alone, Genna turned back to him. Her green eyes were stormy, but she kept her voice low. "Do you want me to go?" He sensed her veiled anger but refused to rise to the bait.

"I would prefer that you finish out the week as we planned," he said. "But if you want to leave, I will pay you for last night. You're not a prisoner here."

She hesitated. "You let me believe Camille was in danger. Why didn't you tell me the truth?"

He sat down across from her. The morning sun gleamed across the surface of the heated water, and a light mist rose from the pool. She needed to understand that this was a precarious situation, and he wasn't going to play nice. It was about guarding his country and his own position of power. "Let me be clear. The success of your grandfather's jewelry empire means nothing to me. But my country means everything. I will do anything necessary to protect Lohenberg. If that means hiring someone to take Camille's place, so be it."

Her complexion paled, but she faced him down. "You were using me so no one would know she left you. You lied to me."

"I hired you to stand in for her. I let you believe what you wanted to believe, but I never said she was in danger. You were the one who drew that conclusion." He had no qualms about whatever she'd thought to justify the deception.

"But you didn't deny it." She took a breath and said, "I'm aware that Camille put you in a terrible position. And that you want this to be a temporary arrangement in exchange for money. But I don't know if I can be the person you want me to be. I don't know if I can work for a man who isn't honest with me."

Amadio sensed the vulnerability in her voice and how much she seemed to value the truth. It wasn't at all what he'd expected. It seemed that she was more interested in his character than the money. But he wasn't about to hold her hostage here.

"If you want to return home with the necklace, I'll pay part of the commission remainder for last night, and I won't stop you." He met her gaze openly. Even so, he suspected that she could not afford to walk away. Her hesitation only proved his point. While she might not want to play this role, it was a business transaction that would benefit everyone.

"Or…as promised, I will pay you an additional million dollars for one week of your time." He let her think about the offer, giving her the chance to fully consider the options. "It's your choice."

"Only a week?" she asked quietly, seeming to consider it.

He nodded. Once again, she seemed to grow silent, turning over the idea in her mind. It was clear that she didn't want to play the role, but if she needed the money, there wasn't another choice. And so, he pressed his advantage. "What is your decision?"

She let out a sigh. "Fine. One week."

Amadio hid his own sense of triumph at her agreement. "There will be rules," he said. "First, you must be with me at all times if we are in public."

"Fair enough."

"Second, you will not engage in conversation with diplomats or ambassadors. I will do the talking. You are to smile and say nothing."

"So, I'm to be a decoration," she remarked. "What century is this again?"

Amadio didn't miss the chill in her voice. But she'd already admitted she didn't know how to be a princess. It was better if she remained silent so no one would guess the truth.

"Third, you—" His voice broke off when she dropped her robe, revealing a bright blue bikini.

"I get the idea. I'm going for a swim."

Her body caught his full attention, from her generous curves to the slight dip of her waist. Her skin was pale, her blond hair tousled around her shoulders. He couldn't for the life of him remember what he was about to say. Something about the third rule, whatever that was. Instead, he asked, "Where did you get that swimsuit?"

"I did pack *some* of my own clothes," she admitted. "It's summer, so I thought I might get a little time to relax while I was here. And I definitely want to get a tan." Her lips tightened. "Unless that's against your rules?"

Genna waited for the prince to answer. He was like a machine, polished and made of steel. She knew she meant nothing to him, and neither did Seraphina Jewels. But ever since his father had guessed she was an imposter, Prince Amadio's mood had turned even colder.

She didn't entirely fault the king for his accusations. Though he was sick, he was still looking after his country and his son. But it irritated her that both of them had treated her as if she were a nobody, a gold digger who cared about nothing but profit.

Was there even a man behind Prince Amadio's stiff formality? She'd glimpsed it after he'd kissed her last night. There were moments when he'd seemed to let down his guard, making her wonder what sort of person was behind the princely title. Or what would happen without any rules between them. Did he even know how to relax?

It was doubtful.

"The rules are for your protection," he said. "Within the palace, so long as you keep up appearances, I don't care what you do."

The more she thought about what lay ahead, the more she questioned the wisdom of staying. What did she know about royalty? Nothing at all. She ought to leave this country behind and return to her grandfather's house, where she could lock herself away in her studio with bits of metal and gemstones. That would be the easiest solution. Instead, she was caught in this trap of her own making. She'd made a devil's bargain and risked her grandfather's company in the process.

She went to sit by the edge of the water and slid her legs into the pool. The water was pleasantly warm, and she couldn't wait to swim some laps.

Amadio's expression remained cool, though he didn't take his eyes off her. "What else did my father say to you?"

"He saw me walking outside and asked to join me. I could hardly say no." Her mood grew strained. "For a man who's ill, he certainly has strong opinions."

"He always has."

In some ways, she was beginning to understand why the prince was so rigid. With a father like his, he would never be allowed to loosen up or have fun. But she hadn't missed the prince's reaction when King Stefan had told her about Camille leaving. Despite Amadio's neutral demeanor, the princess's rejection must have hurt. No matter what had happened between them, he didn't deserve to be abandoned like that.

"What did he think of Princess Camille?"

Amadio shrugged. "He knew the marriage was a political arrangement. And it never mattered to him what I thought of her."

That gave her a reason to pause. It seemed strange to imagine a marriage of convenience in this day and age. "So, what did *you* think of her?"

"What I thought of her then and what I think of her now are two different things," was all he would say.

It hadn't been a positive impression, Genna guessed. But there was more to this arranged marriage than she'd realized. It wasn't about his personal desires—it was to maintain the air of stability in his country.

"Was it your father's idea for you to marry her? Or yours?"

"It was my father's suggestion. I agreed to the union as a means toward peace between our countries."

Again, she saw the impassive expression of a man who made decisions for his country, not himself. It made her wonder what his true emotions were and whether he cared about anything at all besides Lohenberg. Or was he trying to gain his father's approval?

"He's rather ruthless, isn't he? I wouldn't exactly call him fatherly." She glanced back at him, and Amadio's expression hadn't changed.

"He taught me how to rule this country. Sometimes that means making difficult decisions for the sake of others."

She was beginning to understand why Amadio never revealed any emotions. He'd been taught to remain cool-headed by his own father.

"How long has the king been sick?" she asked while moving her legs through the water.

Amadio shrugged. "It started during the past year. I've taken on his duties, though I won't formally become king until he passes."

"That must be hard for you, handling all of it alone. Or does he help you?"

The prince shook his head, but there came a faint spark of irony. "He shares his opinions on everything I do."

She could only imagine what the king had to say—especially in a situation like this one. "I suppose he has a definite opinion about Camille now."

"I told him there won't be a wedding, but he doesn't know everything. He blames me for her running away."

Having met the king, she had no doubt of that. "Will you try to find her and apologize?"

His expression turned irritated. "And why would I do that? It was her choice to leave. I've done nothing wrong. Camille left, and there will be no wedding between us."

And now he was back to being the overbearing, dictatorial prince. She stretched and stood up from the side of the pool. "You don't think you should set your differences aside for the sake of Lohenberg?" If he was going to go through with an arranged marriage, it made sense to attempt a reconciliation.

"No." The frigid tone in his voice made it clear that whatever had happened between them, he would not forgive the princess—nor would he take responsibility for his part. Clearly, whatever had caused the rift had been bad.

"In the morning, I will be speaking with the King of Badenstein to set our strategy," Amadio said. "We will discuss the new terms."

"Will you tell him about our deception?" She didn't know if there would be any consequences for impersonating a princess.

He shrugged. "I imagine he already knows. But I don't want you to come with me. It's too dangerous and too easy to make a critical mistake. You will remain here and pretend to be Camille at all times, no matter with whom you are speaking."

"I'm not a child, Amadio. You don't have to talk down to me." She didn't like his imperious tone.

For a moment, he appeared perplexed, as if he hadn't expected her to stand up to him. "I know you're not a child."

"Good." She started to walk towards him, noting the way his gaze passed over her bikini. Was he...staring at her? She bit her lip, feeling slightly awkward. A confident woman might turn back and smile at him. She might flirt and try to get her way. But Genna had no idea what she was doing. She'd never even had a serious boyfriend.

The prince's blue eyes flared with interest, and she felt an unexpected response as she stared back. She had the sudden fantasy of the prince laying her back against one of the lounge chairs and kissing her hard. Against the wet fabric of her bikini top, her breasts tightened. A sudden tingle caught deep within her as the fantasy played out. She imagined his fingers pulling the strings free, his hot mouth fastening upon a nipple.

Her brain warned that this was *not* a good idea to let her mind wander like this. But she couldn't tear her gaze from the handsome prince, and she felt utterly captivated—not to mention flustered. She needed a distraction, something to break the mood. "Is there any sunscreen?"

The prince gaped at her as if he couldn't believe she'd interrupted with such a request. Before he could say another word, she added, "I forgot to bring some, and if I don't put any on, I'll burn to a crisp."

For a moment, his overbearing attitude dropped away, and he stared at her with raw hunger. Her own breath seized in her lungs, and she wondered what was happening between them.

"It's…on the table over there by the towels." He cleared his throat, and she walked toward the table, trying to hide her self-consciousness.

"Thanks." She retrieved the lotion and then sat down on the lounge chair across from him. For a moment, there was silence between them, as if he were trying to remember what to say.

"I will have Johann write a schedule of the events we'll attend together. You'll need more clothes, so I'll send the stylist to you."

"All right." Was it really this hot outside or was it her embarrassment that made her skin feel on fire? The prince had to be dying in that suit. She wondered if he ever enjoyed a swim or did anything to relax.

Once again, he appeared fully distracted by her bikini. Genna turned her back, feeling the nerves creep back on her. She opened the bottle of sunscreen and poured some into her palm. Slowly, she began to smooth the lotion into her skin, but she could feel the heat of his gaze.

This had been a terrible idea. Her imagination conjured up the vision of his hands sliding over her body, slick with sunscreen, and a jolt flooded through her.

She forced the dangerous thoughts away. *Stop it. This is only a temporary arrangement. Don't even go there.* Amadio had been abandoned before his own wedding, and the last thing he wanted was any involvement with her. Likely, he was humiliated and hurt that Camille had left him. There had to be a reason why the princess had fled so abruptly. Running away seemed completely out of character for royalty. It was possible that Amadio had done something to make her upset, but somehow, Genna didn't believe he'd threatened Camille. No, this was something else.

She wanted to ask him why, but his mood was already dark with frustration. The truth would likely come out soon enough.

"I have meetings," he said at last. "I'll see you in two days."

Two days? Did he really plan to drop all contact with her until the next event? If she was supposed to be his stand-in bride, that wouldn't fool anyone. Engaged couples didn't spend days apart. She frowned, wondering if this was part of the problem. Had he ignored Camille for days on end?

"That's not going to work," she protested. "I'm only going to be here for a week. If you're trying to pretend like everything is fine with the engagement, we can't spend all our time apart."

"What are you talking about?" He genuinely seemed unclear about her point.

"Don't you think people will start to wonder about us if we never spend time together?"

"We spent time last night," he pointed out. "That is sufficient."

"Hardly." She regarded him, wondering if he really thought that was enough. "I will keep up the deception as you asked and attend your events," she said, "but if you want people to believe it, there has to be more."

"No," he countered. "You're being paid for your time, and that's enough."

His swift response startled her. "I'm not asking for more money. I'm asking for an hour of your time each day."

"Why would you want that?" His tone held surprise, as if it was the last thing he'd expected.

"You're asking me to surrender my freedom to help you," she answered. "I'll have to be someone I'm not for most of the day. I want one hour to be myself. And during that hour, I want to know who *you* are. Not the prince, not all this—" She gestured toward the palace. "Just you, as a man. It will be more believable to the palace staff if we spend a little time together. I don't think that's too much to ask."

"I don't have an hour to myself," he started to argue.

"Then I think it's time you claimed an hour of your own. Even if it's only for a swim."

His eyes stared at her in disbelief before they turned heated again. She looked away, having no clue how to handle his interest.

Don't get involved, she warned herself. It would be too easy to get caught up in the fairytale. But she wasn't lying when she'd said that she wanted to know who *he* was, not the prince. And one hour a day wasn't too much to ask.

"It's not a good idea. I don't have time," he countered. He was like a caged animal, trapped in a world of royal rules. But it made her wonder...what would Amadio be like if he were liberated from his prison—even for an hour? It might help soften his rough edges.

"Try it for today," she countered. At this rate, she had nothing to lose. "And if you don't like it, you can book my flight home."

He studied her, and she saw a slight glimmer of indecision. Then he masked it, saying, "I have to prepare for my meeting tomorrow. You'll have to find a way to occupy yourself for now. Perhaps the clothes—"

Genna ignored the suggestion. "If you're trying to get rid of me, you could send me sketch pads and pencils so I can work on more jewelry designs."

He shrugged. "Johann can see to it."

At least she would have something to do with her time. But she sensed that he was still worried about something else. "Is there something else bothering you besides Camille? You seem distracted."

"There have been a number of uprisings in the past few days," he answered. "I have troops guarding the area, but there are rumors that some of the Badenstein rebels are planning more raids. I need to ensure the safety of the border checkpoints."

"And you don't want anyone to believe that your alliance with Badenstein is threatened," she finished.

"Precisely."

She nodded. "All right. Do what you have to do. I only ask that, if we're going to pretend to be a couple, you set aside one hour a day with me. It can be at any time you wish."

"I still see no reason for it. At the end of this week, you're going home."

She understood that. He didn't want to be her friend, and frankly, she doubted if the prince even knew how to relax. He was paying her to be his stand-in princess— and yet, when she looked at this man, she saw someone who had locked away his own emotions. He'd almost been abandoned at the altar, but instead of addressing his own feelings, he was ignoring them.

What kind of man was Amadio? Was he truly a prince of ice who didn't care if his fiancée had run away? His relationship with his father seemed just as troubled. The king was enjoying abdicating his responsibilities while still telling Amadio what to do. It seemed that the prince had reasons for shutting out everyone, including her.

But when she looked at him, she saw the eyes of a man who'd been cast aside. When he'd kissed her, it had begun as an obligatory action. Then she'd softened beneath his mouth and had sensed his hidden craving. He yearned for affection, though he hid it well beneath that stern, stiff demeanor.

She tried to talk herself out of it. This was such a bad idea. He wasn't a wounded animal caught in a trap. She couldn't save him, and it wasn't her business. *You can't fix him,* her conscience reminded her. *Don't even try.* Yet, she wasn't the sort of person to just walk away and ignore another person's feelings.

"Just think about it," she finished.

She was about to leave when he reached for the bottle of sunscreen. "You missed a spot."

At his words, she startled. It was the last thing she'd expected him to say. For a moment, she nearly blurted out, *Where?*

But she couldn't bring herself to speak. She glanced into his eyes, and there was no denying the fire within. He looked as if he wanted to tear off her swimsuit and put his mouth on every part of her. Goosebumps rose over her skin at the thought. She hadn't imagined that there could be this much heat between them. But Prince Amadio made her heart beat faster, and it looked as if he were starving…for her.

Where had that come from?

"It's all right," she said quickly. "I'll get it."

She pulled back the bottle and squirted some of the lotion into her palm, reaching back to get whatever part of her back she could.

She could feel him drawing closer, and her heartbeat quickened when his shadow eclipsed her. The sunscreen was slick in her hands, but all thoughts fled her brain when his hands were on her back. His touch stole her breath, and feelings of longing surged from deep within. Though it was nothing more than a simple touch, she'd never imagined her body's response. She closed her eyes, trying to push back the unexpected attraction. The prince was dangerous beyond words, for she couldn't deny the sensual reaction.

A moment later, he took her face between his hands, leaning in. She was caught off-guard and he was staring at her as if he couldn't get enough.

"What do you want from me, Genna?" His voice was husky, and she suddenly imagined what it would be like to have him touching every part of her.

"Nothing," she whispered. "I don't need anything."

But he leaned in closer, and his blue eyes burned with intensity. "Don't you?"

His mouth descended on hers, claiming a kiss in a reminder of what had happened last night. She suppressed a moan, and the heat of his mouth sent a shock of desire through her skin. She kissed him back, not even knowing what she was doing or why.

But dear God, for a man made of ice, this prince knew how to melt her inhibitions. His mouth demanded her surrender until she hardly knew what was happening.

Then he drew back, leaving her breathless. Without another word, he turned and left.

CHAPTER FOUR

Amadio was starting to think this arrangement was a bad idea. Every time he was around Genna, it was as if his brain and his body short-circuited. He wanted to touch her, to slide his fingers beneath the slender strap of her bikini and lower it to bare more skin. Worse, she'd asked to spend time with him. The request sounded entirely too suspicious. He'd hired her for a job, nothing more. There was no reason for them to get acquainted—if anything, he needed to keep his distance.

He didn't know what it was about this woman, but she tempted him beyond reason. She was undeniably beautiful in a classic, patrician way. Her blond hair framed a lovely face, but it was her innocent green eyes that held him captive. She didn't have the jaded, world-weary attitude of Camille. Instead, she appeared fascinated by the world of royalty, almost enchanted. Part of him wondered if she might be trying for more than a week of being his substitute bride—but he was done with women using him.

Over the course of the afternoon, he'd spent hours with his military advisors, tightening border patrols and heightening security. He'd met with the ambassador, listening to the reasons for the rebellion. Several protestors had cut their way through the fences, setting off alarms and alerting the guards.

It was an utter mess.

But from what he'd heard, Genna had successfully played her role. The newspapers had printed stories about their engagement party, and there had been a flattering photograph of her. Johann had spoken highly of her, and it seemed that several members of the palace staff appreciated her courtesies today. She'd even gone to the kitchens to praise the chefs who had prepared lunch.

The stifling atmosphere of the palace had started to shift after only a day, and Amadio didn't know what to think of that. Genna didn't belong here, and she shouldn't be trying to make a place for herself. Yet, he had no choice but to continue the deception a little longer.

He was exhausted, hungry, and troubled by the events brewing. He'd skipped lunch because of all the meetings, and now, a headache was brewing. When he saw her approaching, he wanted to refuse her request for time alone together. He hadn't stopped for a single moment, and more than anything, he wanted to avoid this woman who tempted him.

The kiss haunted him. He'd meant to make a point, trying to drive her away. But she had yielded against his mouth, kissing him back. The slight taste of her had only aroused a thirst, one he could not quench.

As if in response to his imagination, he saw her walking down the hall toward him. She wore a green sundress and sandals with her hair caught up in a ponytail. There was a sense of calm around her, as if she'd spent most of the day in the sun. Her make-up was gone, but even without it, she was beautiful.

"Busy day?" Genna asked. "I guess you could probably use an hour to relax."

"You can have that hour during dinner," he said. "I'll meet you at the dining room later." Avoidance was the best tactic for now.

She smiled at him as they passed one of the staff members and guided him toward the double doors leading outside. "I thought you might say that. Which is why I ordered our dinner as a picnic instead. Come have a glass of wine and some food."

It *did* sound good, but he wasn't going to tell her that. Instead, he held his silence and followed her, his suspicions rising.

Outside, the afternoon light had begun to fade into evening. Genna had set up dozens of candles around the pool. There was a bottle of wine and two glasses upon a small table with a charcuterie plate and fresh fruits.

"What are you doing?" he said. It looked all the world like a scene of seduction, and his mood tightened. "What is all this?"

"You asked me to play the role of your fiancée. And that's exactly what I'm doing." She poured him a glass of chilled Prosecco and held out the glass. "If I were truly engaged to a man who worked all the time, I would drag him away from his desk for a few hours and convince him to relax."

"This wasn't necessary," he started to argue, but she paid no attention.

"Wearing a dress and dancing with you in front of ambassadors and leaders won't convince anyone that I am your fiancée," she said. "If you're always working, and we hardly talk, who would ever believe that we are to be married?"

He paused at that. "Camille didn't live here, either. We saw each other on a few occasions."

Her expression revealed that she didn't think much of that. "And when is your wedding day meant to be?"

"In two weeks," he answered.

She poured herself a glass and clinked it to his. "Well, I suppose we can tell everyone that I took an extended visit to finish making wedding plans." She passed him a plate with cheese, crackers, prosciutto, olives, and grapes. "We can let them believe the illusion while it lasts."

He practically inhaled the plate of food. "And when the illusion ends?"

"I thought you were going to discuss that with the Badenstein king tomorrow, aren't you? I suppose the two of you will figure out how to break the engagement."

That was the plan, but illusion or not, it would be difficult to end their relationship without the media tearing one of them apart. "We will, yes."

Genna refilled his glass of Prosecco and then her own. "Then we'll enjoy the last few days before it falls apart. Cheers."

He drank, but he still couldn't believe that this was all part of her plan to maintain the deception. It felt entirely too real, and he couldn't relinquish his suspicions. She filled her own plate and he added more to his own.

"Did you know that half your staff members have family in Badenstein?" she said.

He didn't, but he pointed out, "They are Lohenberg citizens."

"True. But many of them said how grateful they are that the fighting and protests along the border checkpoints will stop after our wedding." She ate a few grapes, and added, "Be aware that they're all watching you. They knew something was wrong with your engagement before, but a few of them said to me that they're glad things are better between us."

"But they aren't," he pointed out.

She sat across from him and nodded. "But they *believe* it is, and isn't that what you wanted?"

Genna had a point, though he didn't admit it. She took another sip of her Prosecco and asked, "What are you asking the King of Badenstein to do now?"

"I will order him to remove his troops and put an end to the fighting. Lohenberg will claim the disputed territory since the princess broke our agreement."

"And if he refuses?"

Amadio met her gaze. "Then it will be war between us. And Lohenberg will win."

She let out a slow breath of air. "That's what I was afraid of. People on both sides will be hurt."

"Camille is to blame for that."

"But it's your orders," she argued. "What about your people and their family members? Do you really want to endanger them?"

He understood her point, but it was more complicated than that. He would not stand down in this. Once the media learned that Camille had abandoned the marriage, the tabloids would turn vicious. No one would ask why she'd left—it would be assumed it was his fault.

He didn't want violence—but neither could he afford to appear politically weak. As far as he could tell, there was no other solution. "I'll know more tomorrow."

She set down her glass. "I suppose so." Then she went over to one of the lounge chairs and returned with one of his bathing suits. "I asked Johann to get this for me. Will you join me for a swim?"

"I don't think so. There's still a lot of work I need to do."

"In forty-two minutes, you can go back to work," she said, handing him the suit. "The exercise will make you feel better."

He couldn't remember the last time he'd swum laps in the pool. But perhaps she was right. A swim might help to clear his head. He took the suit and went into the pool house to change. As he did, he thought of Genna's comments regarding his household staff. Perhaps her attempts at being kind could have a positive effect on the gossip.

After he returned from the pool house, he saw that she was back in her blue bikini. She was seated on the steps of the pool, her body partially submerged in the water. For a moment, she was pensive, studying the castle. There was no trace of greed in her expression, only wariness.

It was more difficult than he'd ever imagined to tear his gaze away from her. Instead, he stood on the opposite side of the pool and dove in. The cool water helped push back the frustration of the day, and he swam hard strokes across the water. To his surprise, when he reached the shallow end and turned over, Genna joined him. Though she didn't swim as fast, she cut through the water in smooth laps. Over and over, he swam until he could feel the tension starting to ease.

And when he stopped swimming at last, Genna held out her hand and he took it.

༖

This was not going to be an easy week. She was holding the hand of a gorgeous prince, pretending to be his fiancée. Already, she was fascinated by Amadio, wanting to know more about the man behind the prince.

"Come on. I know what will make you feel better," she told him, leading him towards the spa. Along the way, she grabbed the bottle of Prosecco and brought it with them. "Hot tub."

The water was searing, but it felt amazing after the cool swim. She smiled and leaned back against the jets. Amadio sat across from her, silent and pensive. Genna took a sip directly from the bottle and passed it to him. He drank and then set it down on the ledge between them.

"This is nice," she said. The hot tub bubbles rumbled and tossed between the jets while steam rose from the surface.

Amadio nodded but remained quiet. She waited to see if he would speak, but instead, he closed his eyes and leaned back. Part of her wondered if this was the first time he'd taken a moment to relax. He seemed to be constantly working.

She wanted to talk to him, to somehow break through that invisible wall shielding him from the world. Though she had already decided to stay the rest of the week until he could break the engagement quietly, she didn't want it to be so strained between them. Instead, she wanted to be his friend.

It was probably unrealistic, though. She knew better than to imagine that this was anything more than an arrangement, even after he'd kissed her. It had the angry kiss of a man trying to push her away. Likely he'd forgotten it already. Not that she could. The blazing heat of his mouth had drowned out her reservations, making the rest of the world crumble away until there was only this man. But then he'd ended the kiss, reminding her that she didn't belong in his world. This was only temporary, and she couldn't let herself believe in fairytales.

He was doing everything he could to hold his country together while Camille had run away, leaving him to handle the mess. It would make anyone frustrated and angry. But she couldn't help but see the King of Badenstein's perspective. He wasn't to blame for his daughter's actions, and sending their countries into war over disputed territory wasn't fair to the people. She wished there was a way to stop the violence before it happened.

An impulse came over her, and without thinking, she splashed Amadio. Instantly, his eyes flew open and he stared at her in confusion. "What are you doing, Genna?"

"Something I'll bet you've never done in your entire life." She flicked him with another soft splash of water. "Playing."

For a moment, he looked as if she'd lost her mind. Maybe she had, but she wanted to coax a reaction from him. With a teasing smile, she flicked him again. "Loosen up, Amadio."

A moment later, he splashed her back. The water was hot, but not so bad that it burned her. She laughed and swatted more of the water at him, dampening his hair.

"Water games are for children," he pointed out.

"Maybe so, but when was the last time you indulged in something fun?" She rose up to her knees on the seat of the hot tub. "You work too much."

"I have a great deal of responsibilities. I don't have time to indulge in playing."

With that, she splashed him again. "You have half an hour left to play. Humor me."

In answer to that, he lunged at her, soaking her with hot water. She came up sputtering, even as she was laughing. "That's better."

There was a flicker of a smile at his lips. "I won."

She answered his smile. "You know, taking time to relax gives you a chance to breathe. You'll be a better leader if you're not so tense all the time."

"And you think splashing in a hot tub qualifies to ease my tension?"

"It might. Or there's something else that might help." She sensed that she was treading on dangerous ground with him. But beneath his rigid demeanor, she'd glimpsed a man who was hungry for affection.

"Turn around," she ordered. He looked as if he

wanted to protest, but after an initial hesitation, he obeyed.

She moved closer, kneeling on the seat and reached up to his tight shoulders. The moment her hands were on him, he flinched.

"Relax," she said softly. She knew that this was crossing another boundary between them, but she was caught up in the impulse. Slowly, she began to knead the tension from his shoulders and neck. A bead of water slid from his hair, and she watched it slide down his broad back. She followed its path, massaging him.

She knew this was going too far, but the urge to touch him was too strong. She couldn't deny her own attraction, even knowing that it would end. And likely it was too much, too soon. She didn't have much experience with men to know whether this was a mistake. All her life, she'd been overprotected, feeling so out of place. Her grandfather had loved her, but he hadn't really understood her loneliness.

She could sense the loneliness in the prince, too. He was drowning in it. He isolated himself from his staff, and it was clear that he was also avoiding his father.

Genna continued to run her hands over his neck and shoulders, easing the knotted muscles as best she could. "There. Is that better?"

To her surprise, he turned and caught her wrists. His blue eyes held her captive, and her heart began pounding. "What do you think you're doing, Genna?"

She didn't answer. There really wasn't an answer except that she'd given in to her impulse. "I'm sorry," she whispered, even though she wasn't. "It was just meant to help you relax."

He leaned in closer. "Don't play games with me. This isn't real, and you know it."

She nodded, though he evoked a fierce desire that flooded through her body. When she was near the prince, it was as if all her common sense disappeared. In his eyes, she saw the reflection of herself—someone locked away from the outside world. Someone who dreamed of a very different life, one where someone cared about her.

Right now, she wanted to push back the feelings of being alone. And though it was a risk, she put her arms around his neck and kissed him.

Just as she'd hoped, Amadio claimed her mouth, trapping her against the edge of the hot tub. She didn't care that she would be out of his life in a week. This was about taking a moment for herself. She tasted the Prosecco on his lips, and when he moved his mouth to her throat, she exhaled sharply. He was starving for her, just as she was for him, both of them treading on the edge.

"Was this what you wanted?" he demanded against her skin. He kissed her neck, and heat blasted through her skin. She arched back, shuddering at the intensity of his touch. Never in her life had she experienced such an all-consuming need. She pulled his mouth back to hers, surrendering as he took from her.

Amadio's hands moved down to her waist, and he pulled her onto his lap. She could feel the rigid length of him, and though she was afraid, she ached for more. She traced the line of his shoulders, feeling the ridged muscles.

His kiss gentled, and somehow, the teasing sensation

heightened her desire. He tempted her with the promise of more—but she knew she would never have him. The kiss was only an escape, a silent surrender to unspoken need.

Even though this was temporary, was it so wrong? She touched him, moving her hands up his chest as he continued to kiss her. His hands clasped her waist, and she felt the sleek touch of his tongue probing at her mouth. Genna opened to him, and the sensual onslaught echoed between her legs. She craved more, though she knew it would never happen. He'd given her a taste of the forbidden, making her vulnerable.

Abruptly, Amadio pulled away and sat across from her. His blue eyes had darkened in the sunset, and there was no mistaking his anger. "Don't try to use me, Genna. Though I might enjoy this…distraction…" His gaze drifted over her body "…it's not going to last." He rose from the water and climbed out of the hot tub. "And the hour is over."

He returned to the pool house to change, leaving her to wonder if she'd only imagined the heat between them. She remained in the hot tub, feeling the sting of rejection.

What did you think would happen? That he'd be interested in you? He only wants to keep up the deception. She knew better than to imagine it was more than that. This attraction meant nothing to him.

Genna closed her eyes, realizing how naïve she'd been. She'd let herself get caught up in desire, but real life wasn't like that. She hardly knew the prince, and of course he would believe she was trying to use him. He was probably accustomed to women throwing themselves at him, hoping to marry a prince. He'd never even consider the truth—that she'd been enjoying his company.

Her cheeks burned with humiliation, and she climbed out of the hot tub. It had been a mistake to ask him for an hour.

She wrapped herself in a fluffy robe and decided to try calling her grandfather again. He hadn't picked up the phone earlier, but he needed to know what was happening and why she had changed her plans. After six rings, the call went to voice mail again. Her grandfather rarely answered the phone, so she left him a message, hoping he would call her back.

She took a drink from the bottle of Prosecco and ate some of the leftovers from their picnic. The sky was darkening, the sun rimming the horizon as it descended. She turned her thoughts away from her embarrassment and focused on the positive.

For this week, she could live the life of a princess. After that, she would have more profits to bring to Seraphina Jewels. She ought to be satisfied with that. This was an adventure, a once-in-a-lifetime experience to savor.

And yet...the amount of money felt almost like a bribe. She didn't like taking it from him, nor did it feel right to lie in public about who she was.

"Your Highness?" a voice said. Genna turned and saw one of the footmen holding a cordless phone. "You have a phone call from your father. He wasn't able to reach you on your mobile."

Her father? For a moment, she wondered if he'd meant her grandfather. But then she realized he was talking about the King of Badenstein. Genna stared at the phone, wondering what she was supposed to do. If she said the wrong thing, she could cause a terrible mess. She should make up an excuse not to talk to him… anything really.

But curiosity got the better of her. She thanked the footman and took the phone, praying she wouldn't screw this up. She spoke the Badenstein language, saying, "Yes?"

"What's going on, Camille?" came a clipped voice. "You're not answering your phone. Amadio said that you've called off the engagement, and he told me not to come to the party last night. But I saw a photograph of you dancing with him."

"There have been some complications," she said quietly. "We will discuss it in the morning."

She sensed the king's fury over the phone. "Camille, your behavior has caused even more trouble. You cannot threaten this alliance."

Genna was careful to keep her voice even. "Again, we will discuss it in the morning. Good night." She ended the call, feeling shaky as she did.

She didn't know if she'd pulled off the deception or not. The king hadn't seemed to notice if her voice was different. Perhaps he'd wanted to believe it was her.

Amadio needed to know about this call. She didn't bother changing out of the robe, but she put on sandals before she returned to the palace. On the way, she gave the phone back to the footman as she passed him, thanking him. He inclined his head, and she went up the stairs of the terrace. She had a vague idea of where Amadio's bedroom was, but she wasn't entirely sure.

Genna saw another servant bringing another tray with more food, and she followed him down the hallway.

"Is Prince Amadio inside?" she asked before he could knock at the door.

"Yes, he is, Your Highness."

"Good. I will take him the tray." She knocked on the door and took it from him before he could protest.

"As you wish, Your Highness."

She heard Amadio calling out for her to enter, and she balanced the tray while turning the knob. He was seated at a desk with papers in front of him, along with a map. On the corner of his desk, he had a small monitor with the news on in the background.

"Just put the food on the table," the prince ordered, not looking up from his papers.

Genna obeyed and then closed the door behind her. "I thought you should know that the King of Badenstein called me."

Amadio set his pen down and turned to her. "I'm sorry, what was that?" He blinked a moment, confused as to why she was here.

"The king accused me of not answering my mobile, and he saw the newspaper picture of us dancing last night," she explained. "That's why he called me."

She remained on the far side of the room, and Amadio rose from his chair to cross the room. "You shouldn't have taken his call."

"Well, that *is* what you hired me to do. To take Princess Camille's place. So, I did." She deliberately kept her voice calm. The last thing she wanted was for him to imagine that she had come here seeking more from him.

Genna straightened her posture and regarded him. "He was demanding information about our engagement— whether it was on or off. I told him we would discuss it in the morning." With a shrug, she added, "I just thought you should know."

Before she could turn and leave, he asked, "Does he suspect who you are?"

"I don't think so. I ended the call quickly." She had come with the intention of giving him the information and then leaving, but then she saw a short news segment about the prince's impending marriage. She saw a photograph of Princess Camille, and another of Amadio. Both appeared deeply unhappy.

The newscaster continued, saying, "But conflicting reports suggest that Princess Camille has called off the wedding."

Amadio reached over and turned off the news. She could see in his face that he didn't want to hear anything further. If the media was reporting trouble, it was only a matter of time before he drew criticism for Camille's departure.

"Did something happen today?" she asked. "You seem upset."

"It's nothing you can fix. Don't concern yourself."

"I know, but sometimes it helps to talk about a problem. Even if I only listen."

For a moment, Amadio seemed to be weighing a decision. Then he sighed and beckoned for her to come forward. He pointed to the map he'd been studying. "There was another attack today. Someone set off tear gas near the main checkpoint." He showed her newspaper clippings revealing photographs of protesters.

"What will you do?"

"I'll send more troops to protect the area. But the borders between Lohenberg and Badenstein have always been too fluid."

"Wouldn't it be easier for you if people could easily travel back and forth? Especially if they have family members in each country," she suggested. "Can't you just eliminate the gates?"

"It used to be that way during the nineteenth century. It was peaceful and prosperous for everyone," he said. "But the border checkpoints were built during the Cold War. We planned to get rid of them, but the constant uprisings have made it impossible. My marriage agreement was supposed to bring back peace so we could allow people to travel freely."

"Can't you still negotiate? Why do you have to marry?"

"Because King Heinrich wasn't willing to adjust the terms. He has an outdated notion that our children would have reigned over both countries. He didn't want to give up any territory. An arranged marriage was the easy way out."

The solution was archaic, but she understood why Amadio was willing to consider it. "And what about now?"

He was still staring at the map. "As I said before, Camille broke the terms of our contract, so Heinrich will have to surrender the border lands to Lohenberg."

"I don't think he's going to give up so easily," she said quietly. Any man who thought he could arrange his daughter's marriage in the twenty-first century wasn't exactly forward-thinking. "Especially since you're asking him to take the blame for his daughter's actions."

"I'm going to send troops to protect the border check-points," he admitted, "regardless of what he says."

Which would likely make the king even more suspicious. She decided to try a different tack. "What does your father think you should do?"

"He told me that the fate of Lohenberg is my responsibility. I don't doubt that he has his own ideas, but I'd rather make my own decisions."

Having met King Stefan, she understood Amadio's situation. She had a feeling that the king was constantly testing his son, judging his choice. Despite Stefan's failing health, there was nothing wrong with his mind.

"I have an idea," she said. He turned and gave her his attention. "Tomorrow, I think we should drive together to the borders of Badenstein and be seen by the people. Let them believe the marriage is still happening. It might stop the violence."

"That's not safe for either of us," he argued.

"You mentioned a greater military presence around the borders. Your soldiers would guard us as we drive into Badenstein. We could stop and wave at the people or greet them. It will also send a message to the protesters about your military strength. They might back down and leave the borders."

He remained silent for a time. "Genna, what are you doing?"

"What do you mean?" She saw the suspicion rising in his expression. "It was just an idea."

"I asked you to stand in for Camille. But you cannot take her place."

She paused for a moment, realizing the implications

of what he'd believed. Did he think she was trying to become his princess in reality? That she was wanting to marry him?

"Whoa, hold on. That is *not* what I meant at all. It was just an idea to stop the protests, nothing more." Her embarrassment intensified, though she realized he might mistakenly believe that she was trying to win his heart. "I'm well aware that I'm only here for one week. And no, I don't know how to solve your country's problems. But I was just offering a suggestion."

He stood from the chair. "It's not your responsibility."

"I know. But if smiling and waving from a car will stop people from getting hurt, why not try it?"

He sighed. "Because it will be that much worse when you leave. After I call it off, I will be blamed."

She was starting to sense what he was talking about. And given how cool and composed Amadio was, the media might believe that he'd driven her off. He needed to appear more human in public, like a man who cared about his people. Then, they would blame her and not him.

But changing his image would take more time than she had. He might not want to let the world see him for the man he was.

For that matter, even *she* didn't know what sort of man he was. All she knew was that his entire life was focused upon protecting his country. He was fiercely loyal to Lohenberg in a way no one understood. And she found herself wanting to help him since the king had left him to rule alone.

"I know that I said I wanted you to take Camille's place," he said. "But I only meant in a way that would deter questions from the media. I never intended for matters to become…personal between us." He kept his gaze fixed upon the map, not meeting her gaze. "It was about image management. Nothing more."

Oh. He was talking about the kisses they'd shared, and her embarrassment only deepened. "I suppose you think I'm throwing myself at you," she said quietly. "That's not it at all."

He paused and turned to look at her. "You arranged for candles and Prosecco. You offered me a massage and kissed me in the hot tub. What else am I to think?"

Embarrassment flooded through her, and her cheeks burned with heat. "Okay, so I overstepped. I got a little carried away with making it look romantic, but I only wanted you to loosen up and have fun." It was painful to confess the truth, but she forced herself to continue. "Believe me, I know that you don't want someone like me. I may look like Camille, but I know nothing about being a princess. I get it." He was staring at her, still not speaking, and she felt the humiliation wash over her. "I'm sorry. You hired me to be a stand-in, and that's all you want."

He gave a single nod, and she tried to push back the hurt. "It's better to keep our personal lives separate from this role, Genna."

He was right. She was letting herself get too close, and it would only cause her to be hurt. The prince wanted to end his engagement, conquer the border territory, and live alone.

"All right," she whispered. She took a step backwards and said, "Just let me know if you need me to make an appearance tomorrow."

Amadio's gaze fixed upon her face, and his piercing blue eyes held no emotions at all. "That won't be necessary."

She forced herself to walk away, realizing what a mistake she'd made.

CHAPTER FIVE

Amadio sat in the back of his sedan with Johann Sichermann while the driver approached the borders of Lohenberg. His tension heightened when he saw hundreds of people lining the streets. Some were in cars, some on foot. The border crossing was tightly guarded, with a gate across the road. Though he wanted to open the borders, it was too dangerous right now because of the risk of rioters bringing attacks inside Lohenberg.

They passed through the checkpoint and he thought again of Genna's suggestion, to greet the people and behave as if nothing were wrong. If she were truly going to be his bride, he might have done it. Yet he sensed that the uprisings would only increase after they parted ways.

He'd hurt her feelings last night, but there wasn't a choice. She was getting too close to him, and he'd needed her only for the chance to formally end the betrothal. At the end of the week, she would return to her home, and he would maintain his father's reign over Lohenberg alone.

And yet…he couldn't deny that Genna intrigued him. When she'd kissed him, there was an undeniable attraction pulling him closer. Her impromptu outdoor dinner and the swim had only made it worse. A part of him wanted to believe that her interest was real. He'd known too many women who had used him, playing the role of adoring lover, only to leave and sell their stories to the tabloids when he didn't offer to marry them. With Genna, it was different. They had made an agreement up front. She knew what she was getting, and it gave him the opportunity to hold all the power.

But he'd never imagined that he would enjoy spending time with her.

There was a spirited optimism about her, and she seemed to genuinely want to help Lohenberg. It made him wonder about her past and why she resembled Camille. Just this morning, he'd received an email confirming that the investigation had begun. There were no birth records of her in the state of New York. He might not get the answers he wanted before it was time for her to leave.

But even if she was a distant relative of the princess, what good would it do? Any connection would likely be an embarrassment to King Heinrich.

Amadio stared outside the window as the rolling green hills sped by. It would be a few hours before he arrived at the palace, but he paused to think about his options. After he and Heinrich reached an agreement, they could host a press conference and call off the engagement, stating that it was no longer necessary for a political marriage because their goals had been achieved.

He could script what Genna would say, and they could pull off the façade of friendship.

Amadio broke the silence and asked Johann, "Do you think I made the right choice to leave Miss Hamilton behind?"

The Lord Chancellor shrugged. "We won't know that until you speak with the king, Your Highness. But she would have been interrogated, and the staff at the Badenstein palace would notice a difference in her behavior."

"And what does our staff think of her? Have they guessed that she's not Camille?"

Johann shook his head. "If they have, they've said nothing. They think she's wonderful. She's already learned the names of most of the staff, and she greets them and finds a way to compliment them. Camille never bothered."

Amadio gave a nod, and they continued the rest of the drive in silence.

A few hours later, a footman led Amadio into a small meeting room where King Heinrich was waiting. The older man had dark hair shot with gray, and his green eyes sharpened with annoyance. "Where is she?"

There was no question he was referring to Camille. "She is still in Lohenberg," Amadio answered. "I asked her to stay behind so we could speak alone."

"She is my daughter, and you have no right to—"

"Again, I insist that this conversation be a private one. Tell your advisers to leave. This is a matter that only concerns us."

The king's irritation heightened, but at least he obeyed. Once the room was empty, Amadio signaled for Johann to stand at the doors outside.

The king did not invite him to sit, but Amadio hadn't planned on a courteous meeting. Instead, he unfolded a newspaper he'd brought with him and held out the photograph that had been taken the night of his engagement party.

"Yes, I already saw the photo," King Heinrich said, dismissing it with a hand.

"It's not Camille." Amadio continued to hold out the newspaper clipping. He saw the flicker of concern on the king's face before the older man took the paper and studied it closer.

"What do you mean, it's not Camille?"

"Just that. I hired her to take Camille's place at the party. Have you been in contact with your daughter?"

"I spoke with her yesterday," he snapped. Then he paused a moment and realization dawned. "Unless that wasn't her. I put in a call to your palace when she wasn't answering her mobile phone."

"That was Miss Genna Hamilton," Amadio said. He dropped the newspaper on the coffee table and regarded the king. "Your daughter went away to Italy. The last time I spoke with Camille, she informed me that she was pregnant. I can assure you, the baby's not mine."

The king's complexion drained of color. Amadio said nothing, allowing the truth to sink in. For a long time, Heinrich remained silent.

"The wedding will not take place," Amadio said at last. "But since your daughter broke our agreement, I am here to discuss how we are going to publicly end it."

He laid out his plan for open borders with Lohenberg taking possession of the land, and he ended by saying, "If you accept my terms, Miss Hamilton will publicly hold a press conference and we can end the engagement amicably. If you refuse, the entire world will know of your daughter's behavior and her pregnancy."

He met Heinrich's gaze, and the king's expression hardened. "Just who is this woman posing as my daughter?"

Amadio shrugged. "She's an American jewelry designer. She was here to deliver a diamond necklace that was meant as a wedding gift to Camille."

"And she just *happens* to look identical to my daughter?" the king mused.

He didn't take his eyes off Heinrich. "I think you're the only one who knows why there is an American woman who looks identical to your daughter. And I assume you're wise enough that you don't want others to learn about her existence."

The king said nothing, but his pallor had made him look older than his years.

"I will give you a few days to consider my proposal. In the meantime, Genna will continue in her role, posing as Camille."

With that, he turned and left the room. He had dropped his gauntlet, and now, it was up to Heinrich to make the next move.

"We have a problem."

Genna turned and saw King Stefan approaching. The older man looked weak and pale, but he continued leaning on his cane until he reached her side. She set aside her sketchbook and asked, "What is it?"

"Amadio went to Badenstein today. He won't return until tonight, but there are more people protesting at the borders."

She still didn't understand what he wanted from her, but he said, "You're about to earn your million dollars, Miss Hamilton. Tell your stylist to help you choose an appropriate outfit. You're going with me to the borders, and we're going to put an end to the protests. Right now."

She stared at him, filled with disbelief. What exactly did he expect her to do? "I don't understand. The prince ordered me not to speak to anyone." The last thing she wanted was to undermine his fragile peace. Not to mention, speaking in public terrified her. The very thought made her skin grow cold.

"And as the king, I am changing those orders. You're going to talk to the people, as Camille would have done if she were here," the king commanded. "I'll set up a podium and a microphone. You're going to reassure the people that the wedding will take place, and as a show of faith, we'll open the gates for a short time."

Raw panic rushed through her veins. There was no way she could do this. She'd barely made it through the engagement party, and that was only with Amadio at her side. Everyone would be staring at her, and if she misspoke a single word of the language, they would all know she was an imposter.

Unless that was what King Stefan wanted. She swallowed hard at the thought.

"No—I don't think that's a good idea," she said. "You should be the one to talk to them. You're their king."

"And you're a princess. For the time being." From his smug expression, she believed that her earlier belief must be correct. The king wanted her to fail. And given her lack of experience in public speaking, she probably would. Everyone would stare at her. She would forget what to say or say the wrong thing.

Panic caught inside her, strangling her with terror. "It's not a good idea."

"Neither is violence," the king retorted. "But you're going to stop it from happening. Smile, reassure them, and I'll handle the rest."

Another denial rose to her lips. "I'd rather wait for Amadio," she insisted. "He should be there with me."

"There's no time for that." The king's expression darkened. "But if you'd rather not speak, I'll arrange your flight home. It's your choice."

She was starting to wonder if this was his way of getting rid of her. This was his country, not hers. As the king, he knew exactly what to say and do. But it was now clear that he wasn't her ally and would not support her in any way.

Before she could say another word, he finished with, "You have thirty minutes to be dressed and ready." Then he turned and left.

She gripped her hands together, feeling dazed at what he'd said. The king had always treated her like temporary staff member, someone paid for her time.

But this went beyond anything she'd ever expected. Why was he attempting to throw her into the public spotlight? He'd said he wanted her to reassure the people and try to avoid violence.

She would be photographed, and every word she spoke would be on camera. Was that part of his plan?

The stylist arrived to help her adjust her makeup and brought a new outfit with her. But while Genna transformed into someone else with perfect hair and clothes, she felt her nerves intensify. This was what being a princess was truly about. It wasn't about wearing designer clothes or jewels or even living in a palace. It was about recognizing the needs of people—speaking to them about their problems and reassuring them that the leaders would solve them.

You're not a princess, she reminded herself. *And soon, everyone will know it.*

Her doubts multiplied within her as she got dressed. Every part of her believed that she was about to be forced out of Lohenberg. Amadio would be furious with her and with his father. And she didn't want that.

She liked the prince far too much. Although she understood his reasons for not taking her with him, she would have much preferred to be at his side. He might be reserved and cool on the outside, but she'd glimpsed the fire of the man beneath. Despite all the reasons why this was a bad idea, she started to consider what she might say to the people. She thought about the palace staff members and what concerns they might face. No one wanted violence, and perhaps if she could reassure them that they would work together for a compromise, it might help.

"We should add a necklace to this dress," the stylist was saying. "Emeralds, if you have them."

"Wait a moment." Genna stood from the dressing table and rummaged through her personal belongings until she found a silver necklace with elaborate twists surrounding a simple emerald. She'd designed the necklace herself, and it would complement the dress. She added a matching bracelet and silver earrings before she gathered her courage and went to join the king.

During the car ride to the borders, King Stefan remained silent, staring outside. She didn't attempt conversation, for she knew he wasn't going to help her in any way. Her stomach twisted with fear, and she felt the nerves gathering inside her like a brewing storm. She pushed them back, still mentally rehearsing what she might say.

The sedan pulled to a stop, and she saw hundreds of people gathered at the checkpoint. True to his word, the king had arranged for a podium and a microphone on a raised platform a few hundred feet beyond the gates. From there, she could see the protestors and the crowd.

The driver opened her door, and she stepped outside. Then she turned to the king. "Aren't you going to join me?"

His smile grew sly. "No. I'm going to watch and listen. Unless you want to back down and go home?"

She wanted that more than anything, but his doubts only deepened her annoyance with the king. He was practically daring her to walk away. And something about his demeanor irritated her. No, she wasn't a princess, and she didn't know anything about public speaking. But she also wasn't a quitter.

Genna prayed the rising nausea would stay down long enough for her to get through this. She walked slowly in the heels, noticing how the noise level began to die down. With every step, her knees grew weaker. If she wasn't careful, she might pass out.

And then, from across the border, she heard the sound of cheering.

It was so unexpected, she nearly faltered on the steps, but she caught herself from falling just in time. Why were they cheering for their princess?

Cameras flashed everywhere, and she felt the last of her courage evaporating. She'd never stood in front of so many people. And here she was, an American jewelry designer, pretending to be a princess. It was so wrong.

Genna walked up to the microphone, afraid beyond anything she'd ever imagined. She didn't know what she was doing or what he could say. The king had given her no help whatsoever.

"Good afternoon," she said in their language, praying she wouldn't say the wrong thing. Although she was grateful that her grandfather had taught her to speak the dialect since childhood, she still didn't entirely trust herself. There could be slight differences in the spoken language of the two countries.

The people quieted, and their silence made it even more difficult. They were waiting for her to say something meaningful, and during the slight pause, her panic erupted. She couldn't remember anything of what she'd planned to say. Her mind went utterly blank.

When she glanced over at the king, she saw that he'd fully expected this. A part of her wanted to run from the podium and get back in the car. But then, she saw the face of her driver. It made her remember all the staff members she'd spoken to in the palace, and she tried to imagine their faces upon the faces in the crowd. Maybe if she pretended to speak to them, instead of strangers, she could find the right words.

"I know there has been a great deal of frustration for you," she began. There were a few nods among the bystanders, which was encouraging. Though her hands were shaking, she clenched the edge of the wood, trying to calm herself.

"Many of you find it challenging to visit your friends and families who live on opposite sides of this border." There were more murmurs of agreement. She grew reassured that she was, at least, addressing their concerns.

Her nerves tightened, and below the podium, her knees began to shake. But when she looked into the faces of those standing closest to the podium, she saw that they were listening. They *did* need to hear that someone cared about them. And if nothing else, she could assure them that Amadio was working on their behalf.

"You may have noticed that I have been living in Lohenberg during the past few days," she began. "This has been deliberate, because Amadio and I are discussing ways that our countries can come together. We want peace. We want you to be able to travel freely, to be with the ones you love. And I promise that we will do everything we can to make that happen very soon."

There were nods and even some light applause erupting from the protestors. She turned serious, then. "But I have something to ask of you, in return.

Allow us the time we need to create compromises. Meet us halfway by returning to your homes and allowing us to open up the gates. The protests and the violence are doing more harm than good. Because of this, we are having to increase our security presence with troops. We cannot, and we will not, allow harm to come to our citizens from either country." With that, she thanked them and ended her speech.

A dark sedan drove up to the gates, but the driver stopped and the door opened. To her surprise, she saw Amadio walking toward her. Two guards flanked him as he passed. The people started to murmur, but soon they began applauding at the sight of him.

Genna pasted on a smile, but she knew the prince would be furious with her for speaking. He likely thought that this had been her idea, that she'd defied him. But when she saw his face, it appeared utterly neutral. She stepped down from the podium and held out her hands to him in greeting. When he took her hands, she leaned close and murmured in his ear, "Your father forced me into this. It wasn't my idea. Just play along."

He kissed her cheek before taking her arm. The gesture startled her, for she'd expected him to speak to the crowd. Instead, he lifted a hand to briefly wave at the crowd before he escorted her back to his sedan. She could feel the rigid tension in him, though he masked it by smiling, which caused more cheering from the crowd. She followed him along the walkway, and she sensed his eagerness to get her out of there.

Johann Sichermann stepped out of the vehicle and held the door open for her, but after a quiet word from Prince Amadio, he did not return to the car. Genna got inside, and Amadio joined her. The prince waved to the crowd through the open windows, and she did the same until they were away from the border and on the way back to the palace. Only then did the tension come crashing down on her.

"That was awful. I never want to stand in front of that many people again." Genna rubbed at her temples. "Your father forced me into it. It was either that or he planned to send me home today. I probably should have just agreed to go."

Amadio was studying her, but he still didn't speak. She was waiting for him to respond, to say something. But instead, his mood appeared pensive. Finally, after another minute, he asked, "What did you say to them?"

She let out a heavy sigh. "I promised the people that we were working together to bring peace. That soon, they would be able to travel freely through the borders. But I asked them to give us time and stop the protests."

She was expecting him to tell her she'd made a big mistake. Or demand that she return home and leave Lohenberg to him. Instead, his frosty demeanor unnerved her, for she couldn't guess what he was thinking. The silence stretched further until it became unbearable. "Look, I'm sorry if I messed up. I had to come up with something to say, and that was all I could think of. I just tried to be sympathetic to the people. I know I made all sorts of mistakes."

He was silent for a moment. Then he surprised her when he said, "My father was testing you. He wanted to see if you would turn and run."

For a moment, she considered what he'd said. This had been a test?

"Why would he do this?" Had the king been trying to intimidate her? Was he trying to show her the reality of a royal life? That was never what she'd wanted. She was here to sell the necklace and help the prince, nothing more.

"He wanted to see what you would do," Amadio replied. "To see whether you wanted the role of princess."

"That's never what I wanted," she insisted. "I'm here to play a part, that's all." But her heart had begun to beat faster. The king was acting as if he wanted her to remain here longer. She couldn't understand why. He could easily have given a speech and soothed the people's unrest. Instead, he had thrown her into a situation she hadn't wanted.

Or did she?

She'd been terrified of speaking, and even now, she shuddered at the memory. But when she'd looked into the people's eyes, she had witnessed their frustration. And she'd spoken from her heart, wanting them to know that she would try to help.

You don't belong here, her mind warned. *You're not a princess.*

"Should I have gone away, like your father wanted?" she asked softly. "Or do you want me to stay the rest of the week?"

Amadio said nothing, and his rigid posture made her wish she hadn't spoken at all. He was a royal prince, and she was nothing but a girl from upstate New York.

His continued silence only emphasized the truth that they were worlds apart. She could never know what it was like to be royalty, and it hurt to realize that he didn't truly want her here.

"All right," she whispered. "I guess that's my answer then."

To her shock, Amadio took her face in his hands and kissed her hard. His mouth devoured hers, and she was so stunned, her lips opened to him. His kiss was overwhelming, like a man claiming a forbidden temptation. Heat roared through her, and she didn't know why he was kissing her or what thoughts were in his head. There was no reason for him to kiss her, especially now.

Unless he wanted her.

The very thought was such a shock, every thought left her brain. All she could do was rest her hands on his shoulders while she yielded to his mouth. His tongue entered her mouth in a sensual slide that made her body ache for more. Desire burned inside her veins, but it was about more than just physical need. In this moment, she sensed that he was trying to banish demons of his own. As if he could get her out of his head if he only kissed her long enough.

Though she knew she should push him away, she couldn't bring herself to do it. This man was shouldering the burden of a country, and she could feel the tension in him. But despite the initial fervor of his kiss, she reached out to touch his cheek. He gentled the kiss, and when it turned tender, her own inhibitions fell apart. He kissed her like a man craving affection, and the more she gave to him, the more his demeanor shifted.

When the car came to a stop, he tore his mouth from hers. His blue eyes were burning with a dark need, and she didn't know what to say. Her own breathing was unsteady, and she had no idea what he wanted from her. Beneath her palms, she could feel the echo of his heartbeat.

"I'm going to let you go at the end of this week," he said roughly. "This means nothing."

His words felt like a physical blow, and color flooded her face. Was he trying to convince her or convince himself? In only three words, her pride had disintegrated into dust.

The driver opened the door, and Amadio stepped out first. Then he held out his hand to help her. Genna gripped it, feeling as if she might stumble upon the gravel. She didn't know what to think of the sudden kiss, but right now, her anger was rising. Did he think she would simply fall into his arms because he kissed her? That she could be so easily manipulated?

She couldn't deny her attraction to this man, but she also didn't want him to believe she was an easy seduction. Far from it.

He guided her down the long hallway, moving his palm to the small of her back. But when he led her towards the stairs, she stopped him. "What do you want from me, Amadio?"

To her surprise, his expression seemed to soften. "An hour of your time. There's something I want to show you."

It deflated some of her anger, and she followed him up another staircase. Hardwood floors with intricate inlaid patterns lined the hallway, and velvet-covered stools rested at regular intervals beside the doors.

He led to another room at the far end of the hallway, opening the doors to reveal glass windows stretching from floor to ceiling. A crystal chandelier hung above the center of the ballroom. The walls and built-in shelves were white, while the fireplace on the opposite side had a malachite green marble hearth.

But it was the view that stole her breath. The sunset gleamed against the green hills in the distance, and she went to stand before the windows. Amadio opened sliding glass doors that led to the balcony. For a moment, she walked into the evening air, breathing in the scent of stone and ivy. How could Camille walk away and leave all this behind?

"It's beautiful," she whispered. "I can see why you love it here."

Amadio came to stand beside her, and he rested his hands on her shoulders. From deep inside, she felt the invisible pull towards him. Oh God, this wasn't good. She needed to maintain distance between them, or else she might forget that there would never be any relationship with this man.

"It's my responsibility to protect Lohenberg. I will do everything I can for my country." In his voice, she heard the immense loyalty. The feelings he held were real, and it warmed her to hear it.

But she didn't understand what he wanted from her, beyond taking Camille's place. One moment he treated her like a piece of paper, a contract buying him time from the media. Then the next moment, he behaved as if he couldn't keep his hands off her.

She couldn't deny her own confusion. She lacked experience when it came to men, He had crossed the line in the car when they'd been alone, and she wanted to know the truth.

"Amadio, why did you really kiss me?"

He couldn't tell her the full truth. How could she understand that every woman he'd ever known before Camille had been ready and eager to assume the role of princess? They had dated him with the hopes of inheriting a country. Every last one of them would have been delighted to step out on a podium and address a crowd. They would have delivered a careful speech, every word planned. Afterwards, she would have wanted Amadio to be pleased by her performance. For that was exactly what their behaviors had been in public— calculated performances.

His father had always found a way to reveal their avarice, and though Amadio had hated being proven wrong, he knew that Stefan was trying to protect him. The king had attempted to expose Genna as a gold digger today, but instead, she'd revealed her warmth and compassion to the people. Before he'd approached the podium, Amadio had heard the last part of her speech, and though her voice had trembled, her words had been kind. Her reluctance to speak had revealed her vulnerability, but more than that, she had been trying to help suppress the violence. The people had responded to her with applause and support.

For the first time, he'd glimpsed what it would be like to have an ally at his side. And so, he could only answer her question with honesty. "I kissed you because I wanted to."

It had been an impulse, really. Sometimes, when he caught her looking at him, he wondered if she felt the same attraction he did. Or was she only playing the part for public appearances? She'd kissed him that day they had spent time together in the hot tub, but it could have been a premeditated move. He'd wanted to see how she would react with no warning.

And the answer confused him because she'd kissed him back with as much yearning as he'd felt.

It unnerved him that she looked so much like Camille…and yet, the pair of them could not be more different. Camille had been polished and perfect, trained from birth to be a princess. Genna was nervous and spontaneous with no idea of what she was doing. And something about her inexperience fascinated him.

"You shouldn't have done that." Genna kept her gaze fixed upon the horizon, and he sensed the tension in her body. "Because as you said, I'm leaving by the end of the week."

"You're right." But he reached out to touch her spine and noticed that she wasn't pushing him away. For a moment, she remained frozen in place. Then she turned back to him, resting her palms upon his chest. The scent of her skin made him want to lean even closer, to taste the softness of her neck.

"I know that we have to be a couple in public. But in private, we should only be friends."

"I agree." Then his gaze flickered down to her hands.

Her cheeks reddened, as if she suddenly realized what she was doing. Then, she seemed to gather her composure, and she straightened. "We can't form an attachment, or it will be too hard to let go. It only complicates everything, and it goes against the rules we set up."

He leaned in, his forehead touching hers. He heard the subtle intake of her breath as he offered, "Unless you want to change the rules for a few days." He expected her to shove him away, but instead, her expression grew strained.

"You don't want someone like me."

Amadio lifted his hand into her hair, stroking it back from her face. "As long as you understand that it's not permanent, there's no harm done. What we do in private is no one's business but ours."

He waited another heartbeat before he stole another kiss. He kept it soft, and beneath his mouth he could sense her yielding to him. He wanted this woman, to steal a forbidden touch and perhaps claim her in his bed before she left, if she was willing.

He slid his hands down her body, noting where his touch made her tense. "Because of what you did today, many of the protesters left. Your instincts were good."

"I didn't have a choice."

He kissed the line of her jaw, down to the sensitive place upon her throat. Genna expelled a shuddering sigh, arching against him. Their hips pressed together, and he gripped her waist, letting her know just how badly he wanted her.

"But you did have a choice. You could have left." He continued exploring her skin with his mouth, and then he guided her back inside the ballroom, pulling the door shut behind him. "You have the same choice now."

Her silence revealed her uncertainty, but she didn't protest. He reached for the zipper of her dress and lowered it slightly, peeling back the gown to reveal her bare shoulder. Then he kissed the soft skin of her neckline. Her skin rose up with goosebumps, and she leaned back to rest her head against his face.

"I don't know why I'm here," she admitted. "Except that maybe a part of me wants to imagine that it could be real. Even though I know it's not."

"Do you want me to stop?" he asked.

Her voice was the barest whisper. "I don't know."

He moved his hand lower to cup her breast through the silk of her gown, and she shivered at his touch. The thought of possessing her body, arousing her until she cried out in pleasure, was a challenge he couldn't resist. It had been so long since he'd been with a woman, and even then, he'd known that she'd wanted his title, not him.

He wasn't so certain whether Genna was the same.

Her continued to caress her nipple through the fabric. He could feel the tight bud rising, and she closed her eyes, her face revealing how much she liked his touch. But then, she seemed to gather her composure.

"I do want you to stop," she whispered. Slowly, she took a step back, but the strain on her face was undeniable. "Because I'm not like your other women. I don't want to be used and discarded," she answered. "That's not who I am."

He understood her concerns, but that wasn't what this was about. "It would be about mutual pleasure. We're both feeling immense pressure right now. We could ease each other."

But in her eyes, he saw panic. "I can't. I barely know you." She stepped back and blurted out, "Even if I did, I wouldn't even know what to do…" Her voice trailed off, and then she said, "I'm sorry, I just…don't want my first time to be a casual arrangement. I want it to be with someone I love."

So, she was a virgin. He'd wondered about that. And he understood her hesitation, along with her desire for a committed relationship. It wasn't something they would ever have, so perhaps she was right to end this now.

"I understand." He backed off, giving her space. Her cheeks were flushed, and she reached back to pull up the zipper.

A sudden awkwardness descended and to change the subject, she asked, "What did the King of Badenstein say?"

"He will let me know within a few days. I told him that there will be no marriage."

"And how did he react to that?"

"There's nothing to discuss. His daughter broke the agreement. Therefore, he has forfeited the land."

"But that's just it. His daughter was in the wrong, not him." She shook her head. "I don't think you should blame the king for Camille's mistakes."

"I don't blame him. But he knows there are consequences for breaking a political alliance." He held no sympathy toward the king, nor would he bend. After what Camille had done, *she* was responsible for the outcome, not him. There was no excuse for such a betrayal.

"You would risk people's lives for your own pride?" Genna asked softly.

"Sending more troops to the border to defend Lohenberg is no risk at all. But I will defend the peace." Her expression held doubts, but he refused to bear any guilt. *He* was the wronged party, and Heinrich owed him.

"How do you plan to break the engagement?" she asked. Though she kept her voice neutral, he sensed her disapproval.

"We will have a press conference and make an announcement that we have reached an agreement about opening the borders, and that a marriage is no longer necessary."

He didn't miss the shadowed disappointment on her face. "I know that's what you wanted."

"You don't approve."

She shrugged and shook her head. "I think you're better than this, Your Highness. I don't want to believe that you're a ruthless conqueror who will take from others."

He leaned in and caught her waist. "You're wrong, Genna. I take exactly what I want."

Her face turned stormy, and she gave him a gentle push. "But you won't take me."

CHAPTER SIX

The next day, Genna made an effort to stay away from the prince. She knew where this was leading and wanted no part of it. Amadio had no intention of this relationship becoming real, and her heart would only get broken if she let him get close again. It was one thing to kiss in public, but she had to ensure that it never happened again in private.

In the meantime, she needed to stay busy, to keep her mind engaged and protect her wayward heart. If she didn't reinforce her willpower, she would fall beneath his spell. She couldn't take that risk, no matter how handsome he was.

And so, she'd asked one of the staff members to help her get a sketch book and pencils. Today, she had chosen to sit on a bench in a long hallway that had once been an assembly room. There were dozens of oil paintings hung upon the walls, likely ancestors of the prince.

Genna was hoping to study the jewelry of the princesses, and there had been no shortage of inspiration.

She'd sketched several Victorian necklaces, and there was a pair of ear bobs that fascinated her with twists of gold and garnet stones set within them.

She drew shapes, combining the floral patterns with bolder lines. Inspiration struck, and she got caught up in new ideas. With her pencils, she added colors and subtle shades.

"There you are," came Amadio's voice. He strode into the room, and she tried not to be conscious of his handsome face and the way the lines of his suit clung to his frame.

"Hello," she greeted him, though she didn't look up from her sketches. He came to stand behind her and studied them.

"Your drawings are good."

"Thank you. I'll need materials and tools to make the pieces. I've missed designing jewelry." It was strange to imagine returning to the life she'd had before, working in her studio.

"I'm surprised your grandfather had the money to invest in high-end jewels." He sat beside her, watching as she sketched.

"It took him years to build Seraphina. He moved to the United States before I was born, and I'm told that he used to sell jewels in New York at the Diamond District before he built a name for himself." The thought of her grandfather brought a slight twinge of worry, for he still hadn't called her back.

"Do you make the jewelry yourself or do you only design the pieces?"

"A little of both, depending on how complex it is.

I can't always make what I envision, but I can repair almost anything." She set her sketch book aside, along with the pencils. "Was there something you needed from me? Do we have to attend an event tonight?"

"Possibly tomorrow," he clarified. "But I wanted to talk with you about the king's answer. He called this morning."

"What did he say?"

"He refused my offer, as I expected he would."

She wasn't at all surprised. Amadio had demanded everything in return for nothing. "And what will you do now?"

"I'm going to assemble troops at the border. Once he knows I'm not bluffing, I expect he will back down."

The show of military force threatened to undo everything she'd promised the people in her impromptu speech. She wanted to argue with him, to urge him to wait. But what good would that do? She wasn't the real princess, and it wasn't her place to give Amadio advice. He was the crown prince, and he would never listen to her.

A heaviness settled in her stomach, and she turned back to her drawings, distracting herself with something she *could* control.

"Well?" he demanded.

"Well, what?"

"Do you think the king will surrender the land?"

She set down her pencil and faced him. "No, I don't. I think both of you are behaving like children fighting over a toy."

"You don't understand."

"You're right, I don't. But it doesn't mean I agree

with your choice. You've left him no alternative except war. He will appear weak in front of his people if he doesn't fight back."

"He did have a choice."

"Not if you demanded everything." She packed up her drawing materials and said, "If you truly want a truce, Amadio, then you have to be willing to compromise."

But from the rigid expression on his face, he wasn't willing at all. "You know nothing about ruling a country."

His words were an invisible blow, but she managed a nod. "You're right. I don't." She didn't bother arguing with him, but instead packed up her materials and left.

As she walked down the hallway, she held back her emotions. It was stupid, getting so upset over this situation. It would be over in a few days, and she'd go home to a normal life. But it bothered her deeply that the prince was about to embark on a decision that could cause more protests and violence. He was so determined to gain the upper hand, unwilling to bend.

There's nothing you can do. He won't change. She knew that. And yet, another part of her wondered if she could convince him to compromise. Would Amadio consider it, or was he determined to uphold his pride, even if it meant hurting innocent people?

She knew this wasn't her country. Nor was it her responsibility.

A tightness gathered in her throat as an old memory resurfaced from her childhood. It had been a hot summer day, and she'd been playing on the monkey bars with her best friend.

"You want some gum?" Leah had asked, holding out the pack of bubble gum. Genna had been about to take a piece when Walter Brown had shown up. Walter was taller than anyone else in their fifth grade class and had a reputation as a bully.

"I want some," Walter had said as he came closer. Genna hopped down off the bars and took a step away. He'd always made her nervous.

"I didn't say you could have any." Leah shoved the pack of gum in her pocket and reached for the high metal rungs that stretched like a ladder. She made her way to the middle of the bars when suddenly Walter grabbed her by the legs. She screamed, "Stop it! Let go!"

Genna knew she should step in and help. Maybe push Walter away or do something...anything. But her feet remained frozen in place, and she didn't dare move. Her heart was pounding, and her stomach twisted with fear as she watched him wrench her friend off the bars and shove her to the ground. Leah hit the grass hard and split her lip open.

Walter took the pack of gum from Leah's pocket and strode away, shoving a piece in his mouth as he left.

Never in her life had Genna been so upset with herself. She'd stood by like a coward and done nothing while someone had hurt her friend. She'd been so afraid that Walter would hit her if she tried to step in. Her fear had taken over, and even now after all these years, she despised herself for not trying to help.

And wasn't that what she was doing right now? Standing aside while other people could get hurt?

She set down her pencil and thought a moment. All her life, she'd lived in the shadows, never having much of a love life, and certainly she'd hadn't known what to do when Amadio had kissed her. He desired her—there was no doubt of it—though she had no idea why.

But maybe...maybe she could use that desire to convince him of another way. What if she could soften his anger and make him see another side?

After the playground incident, she'd later learned that Walter had been taken into foster care, away from his parents because of neglect and abuse. He'd probably stolen the gum because he hadn't had enough to eat. If he'd had even one friend to care about him, to help him, he might not have been such a bully.

Genna took a breath, gathering her courage. She couldn't change the past...but it might be possible to change the future and stop the fighting before it began.

All she could do was try.

Despite giving the order to increase the military presence around the borders, Amadio sensed that Genna was right. The soldiers would only ignite the people's anger. But he saw no alternative. If he ignored the terms of his treaty with King Heinrich, his own position grew weak. Once the press learned of the broken engagement, the media would tear him apart if he opened the borders and surrendered half the disputed territory for no reason. His gut soured at the thought.

Even so, he couldn't stop thinking of how his decision had changed Genna's mood...and how disappointed she'd seemed. He shouldn't care what she thought, but she'd eyed him as if he were a heartless monster.

He was going to send her home in a few more days; that was a given. And yet, he remembered how she'd teased him, how she'd created an hour of fun with swimming and the hot tub. When she'd been happy here, she had lifted his spirits, giving him a glimpse of a very different life.

A life he had no right to want.

He had asked for a week, and she'd granted it. Did that make him a bastard, knowing he had to send her back but wanting to enjoy the remaining days? He craved her touch, needed her in a way he didn't want to acknowledge. She had gotten beneath his skin, and a darker side of him wanted to take advantage of her sweetness. He wanted to claim her, giving them both a taste of seduction.

His mobile phone rang, and when he didn't recognize the number, he thought of letting it go to voicemail. But then he decided to answer and was taken aback at the sound of Camille's voice.

"Amadio, we need to talk."

A sudden fury rippled through him, though he tamped it down. There was nothing he wanted to say to her, but somehow, he forced himself to answer, "Go on."

"I am so sorry for all of this. It was never my intention to put you in this position. What happened with Marcus was something I never expected. I felt...so trapped. I had no control over my life. I just wanted to be rebellious and do the worst thing I possibly could." Her voice had gone so quiet, it was barely above a whisper.

"I know you probably never felt a prisoner the way I did. But you didn't deserve any of this."

She was wrong. He knew exactly what it was to be a prisoner, to feel like he had no control over his life or his choices. If he'd had the freedom Camille had seized, he would take Genna away on holiday, somewhere tropical where they could relax away from the public eye.

"Your choices caused chaos," he said.

She fell quiet for a time. "I know. And I saw the photograph of the woman you used to take my place. She does look a lot like me. It was a good idea, but I'm sorry you had to resort to that."

He said nothing, but it was time to take command of the conversation. "Camille, if you were thinking I would take you back, the answer is no. We will not be married."

"No, I didn't expect you would. And especially not now with the baby."

"What do you want from me?" he demanded. He couldn't truly see any reason for this conversation.

"I just...wanted to apologize for all this. It wasn't fair to you."

He said nothing, for he couldn't grant her forgiveness. An apology wouldn't change their circumstances.

"I intend to stay in Italy until the baby is born," she said quietly. There was a heaviness in her voice, and she continued, "After that, I may return to Badenstein."

"And what of the child?"

"I don't know yet." She sounded as if she were holding back tears, but she said, "All I ask is that you try to work things out with my father. Don't let my mistakes cause war between you."

"I've already spoken with him. He refuses to surrender the border lands, so I've increased Lohenberg's military presence."

"Amadio, no. Please don't."

But he saw no reason to continue the conversation and hung up the phone. Amadio took a moment to calm his frustration. Thankfully, he did have Genna to help him continue the ruse, even if she had echoed Camille's concerns about the borders. He appreciated her candor… and a part of him appreciated being challenged, even if he disagreed with her.

His father had essentially abandoned him to make all the decisions. Although Stefan was still the king, his claim to illness had given him the means to step down. A twinge of annoyance caught Amadio, for he wanted to speak to his father and get the advice he needed. Yet, the king had been avoiding a direct answer.

It might be that Stefan didn't know the right course of action any more than he did.

Genna had warned him to compromise, but he didn't see how that was possible anymore. The King of Badenstein had already refused his offer. There was no doubt that she was upset with him for forcing King Heinrich's hand. She had revealed that clearly enough when he'd interrupted her sketching.

A gift might be useful by way of an apology. He suspected that Genna wouldn't want traditional apologies like flowers or luxurious gifts. Instead, he tried to think of what she might appreciate. He thought of her sketches, and an unusual idea occurred to him. Though he didn't know if she would love it or hate it, it was worth a try. With a quick phone call to Johann, he decided to give her something to do—something she might enjoy.

And perhaps she would want to spend another hour with him tonight before the rest of his country fell apart.

"What is this?" Genna asked when Johann held out a cardboard box. She'd been drawing in her room when the Lord Chamberlain had knocked. Well, avoiding Amadio was more accurate.

"His Royal Highness asked that I bring this to you. And I've taken the liberty of providing the tools he requested, as well."

Curious, Genna accepted the box and glanced inside. It took an effort to hold back her gasp when she saw the delicate tiara. "Prince Amadio sent this?"

"He did. He said it might occupy your time. And he said that he would like it if you'd…what was it? Spend an hour with him this evening?" With that, the Lord Chamberlain inclined his head and walked back to the door.

"Will you tell him thank you? And yes, of course I'll join him."

He nodded, pausing a moment. "If you'll forgive me for saying this, Miss Hamilton, you're good for him. We've all noticed how you've eased the tension here."

She didn't know quite what to say to that. Her face seemed to flush, but she thanked him. There wasn't any other answer, for they both knew she couldn't stay.

"Prince Amadio is a strong ruler, and he would do anything for his country," Johann continued. "He asks nothing for himself. And whether you know it or not, you've made this week more bearable for him."

With that, the Lord Chamberlain left. Genna hesitated with the box, and she sensed that she was treading on unfamiliar ground. Why would the prince entrust her with a gift like this?

She lifted the tiara from the box to study it more carefully. Emeralds and diamonds were set all around the piece, but several of the stones were loose. A few diamonds had gone missing from the crown. Inside the box, she found a black velvet bag, along with a selection of pliers. She opened the bag to see the contents and poured out the missing stones into her palm. There had once been pearls in the tiara, she realized, along with the diamonds.

And then she realized what it was. She'd told Amadio she could fix any piece of jewelry, and he'd given her this piece to occupy her time. Did he only mean for her to fix it? Or would she be allowed to keep it? She wasn't quite sure. But the gift felt like an apology for what he'd said. It *had* hurt when he'd claimed she knew nothing about ruling a country. Was this supposed to make it better? It almost felt as if he were trying to buy her again.

She paused and picked up the pliers. No, this wasn't about buying her. If it were, he'd have given her a tiara that needed no repairs. This was something else entirely, especially since he had asked for an hour of her time.

These weren't the right tools, but she decided to begin laying out the missing stones in order while she thought of the best way to reset them.

A knock sounded at the door, and when she called out permission to enter, she saw the prince standing there.

His face held tension, and he appeared hesitant before he stepped inside.

She decided to break the silence and offered, "This is the most beautiful piece I've seen in years. How old is it?"

"It's from 1840, I believe." Though he said nothing else, she detected that he was watching her reaction. She tilted it up to the light, watching the jewels gleam. She hadn't seen emeralds this lovely since she'd viewed one of Queen Victoria's crowns.

"Why did you send this to me? Should I assume that you want me to fix it?"

He paused. "You may, if you wish. But that wasn't why I gave it to you."

An unsettled suspicion crept inside her, making her wonder what his intentions were. He continued by saying, "You've kept your end of the bargain quite well, Genna. Because of your skills, I thought you might be able to repair it. And you may keep it, afterwards. It does have historical value, but of course, no one has worn it in many years. It belonged to Princess Hannah."

She turned back to the tiara, still feeling uncertain about it. Repairing the tiara was a means of occupying her time in a way that would bring her enjoyment, not to mention it was worth a fortune. But she still questioned his motives.

"It's beautiful," she said. "Why didn't anyone fix it before now?"

"The princess locked it away after her husband died. It was a gift from him, and she didn't want to be reminded of her loss. Others believed that it was unlucky."

"You gave me an unlucky tiara?" she mused. With a wry grin, she added, "That explains everything." She'd only meant it in teasing, but he shook his head.

"I don't believe in superstitions. It was given to the princess out of love, and regardless of its reputation, I think it deserves to be restored."

She agreed with him on that point. Something this lovely should never be locked away. And even if she had nowhere to wear it, it would give her a priceless memory of this time with the prince. She could never imagine selling a piece like this—not with the history it held. And he knew it, too.

"Do you have what you need to make the repairs?" he asked.

"Unfortunately, no. I need a jeweler's saw, soldering wire, files, polishing wheels and compounds—" She broke off at his dazed expression.

"Send Johann your list of tools," the prince replied. "He will see to it that you have everything you need." With that, he turned to go, but she wasn't about to let him walk away so fast.

"Amadio, wait."

He paused at the doorway. Though he was still the polished, perfect prince, she had seen another side to him tonight. The tiara had been freely given in an attempt to ease the tension between them, and she wanted to express her gratitude.

Genna closed the distance and reached for his hand. "Thank you. It's absolutely the most gorgeous gift I've ever received. I love it." She squeezed his palm gently, and he froze for a moment. He seemed taken aback by her hand in his, and yet, he didn't let go. Genna grew captivated by the intensity in his eyes and the unmistakable interest. She wanted to loosen that tie, to feel his mouth upon hers again.

Be careful, she warned herself. There was more to this man than she'd imagined, and he was dangerous. If she didn't guard her heart, their arrangement could slip past the boundaries and become something more. Even now, she wanted him to kiss her again so she could lose herself in the fantasy.

But she forced herself to relax her hold as she took her hand away. He was staring at her with those gorgeous blue eyes, and he said only, "Six o'clock. Meet me by the fountain in the gardens."

The hour they would spend together. Though she didn't know what was happening with her wayward feelings, she would not deny him. "I'll be there."

He squeezed her hand and left her alone, closing the door behind him. After he'd gone, she examined the tiara again, sharpening her focus on something else. With the right tools, she could restore it to its former beauty. Yet even as she started to match up the missing pearls to the settings, her mind drifted back to Amadio's dilemma. There was no question that he'd been the victim in this broken engagement. She wished she could somehow help him find a compromise with the king… but she worried that he would never consider meeting King Heinrich halfway.

It's not your business, she warned herself. Yet, how could she stand by and do nothing? She had to find a way to convince Amadio to negotiate, even if that meant interfering in matters she didn't understand.

She set aside the tiara and made two lists—one for

Johann, and the other for the housekeeper. There were some things she needed, not only the tools to repair the tiara, but supplies she wanted for tonight's hour with Amadio. Her method was unconventional, but she had a feeling that his competitive spirit would break through. And once he had lowered his guard, she hoped he might listen to reason.

When Genna arrived, Amadio was surprised to see her carrying a small canvas bag. He wondered why she'd brought it along.

"Hi," she said. "Should I assume we're going for a walk?"

She had guessed correctly, and he nodded in affirmation. "You asked for an hour of my time," he answered. "I'm holding up my end of the bargain."

She looped her arm in his. "Lead on, then."

He took her down a small pathway illuminated by solar lights. The white gravel was easily visible, and he took her toward one of the gardens on the far end of the palace estate. When they arrived, Genna had to duck beneath a boxwood archway. Inside, white blossoms of gardenia, jasmine, and even roses, had begun to bloom.

"This is amazing," she said, reaching out to smell a gardenia flower in a stone urn. "I've never seen a garden all in white."

"It was my mother's moonlight garden," he said. "She designed it herself."

Her smile turned chagrined. "It makes me regret what I brought with me for entertainment. It's completely inappropriate."

"What did you bring?"

She withdrew a bottle of wine and a bottle of whiskey, as well as a selection of plastic cups.

He didn't see an issue with enjoying a glass of wine in the garden, but she set up the plastic cups in a pyramid shape on one end of the low stone wall. Then she opened the bottle of wine and poured most of it into one set of cups. She set up a second pyramid of cups on the opposite side and filled them with whiskey.

"What is this, Genna?"

"I thought you needed to loosen up and have a good time. So, we're playing beer pong. Except with wine and whiskey. And each time you take a drink, you have to answer a question truthfully. Whatever it is."

He blinked at that. If he remembered correctly, this was a game played at university parties. Genna held out a table tennis ball and handed it to him. "Choose which side you'd rather drink."

"I'll take whiskey," he said. "Tell me why we're doing this?"

"Because it's fun?" she suggested. "Try to land your ball in one of my cups. If you do, I have to drink what's inside the cup."

"I don't see why we don't just drink from the cups to begin with." The games seemed little more than an excuse to drink alcohol.

"Where's your competitive spirit?" she teased.

He had no issue at all with competition, but he questioned her motives. "Are you trying to get me drunk?"

"Maybe." She smiled and said, "You go first. I'll bet you can't land your ball in one of my cups."

He took aim at the cups, but his first one bounced off the rim. He gauged the distance and decided to change the angle of his wrist the next time.

"My turn." Genna took aim, but her ball also missed. She handed it back to him. "I always wanted to try this game, but my grandfather wouldn't allow it."

"I'm not surprised." He took aim again, and this time, his ball landed in a cup. Genna took it, lifted out the ball, and drank the contents. Then she removed the cup from the wall.

"All right, what's your question?"

He thought a moment. At first, he wanted to ask about her past, to try to draw a connection between Genna and Camille, but he doubted if she would have any of the answers. Thus far, his private investigator had turned up nothing. Instead, he asked, "Why did you let me kiss you when we were alone in the car?"

She turned the ball over in her fingertips. In the moonlight and the solar lamps, he could see the uncertainty on her face. But then she admitted, "When you're not being so overbearing and demanding, you're an attractive man. And I liked kissing you."

He realized after he'd asked the question that he'd sounded as if he were fishing for compliments. But even so, she'd sounded sincere. He just didn't know what to think about it now.

Genna took aim, and this time, her ball landed in one of his cups. He took it, removed the ball, and drank the whiskey. It gave a pleasant burn down the back of his throat, and he stacked his cup inside the one she had placed on the ground.

"Go on, then. Ask your question." He expected her to ask him about Camille or about Badenstein. Clearly, her game had been a set up for information. He could use that to his advantage if needed.

Instead, she asked, "If you were not a prince, what would you do for a living?"

The question was completely unexpected and one he'd never really thought about. He'd been born a prince, and every choice had been taken from him. Though he lived in luxury, the price was his freedom.

"There must be something you *like* to do," she offered. "Something you've always wanted to try."

"I like to travel," he admitted. "I don't always get a chance to see the world. I'd often thought I would enjoy photography. When I was very young, my mother took me on a trip to Italy. We walked through orange groves and went hiking along the coast. It's one of my favorite memories of her."

Genna smiled and handed him the ball. "That does sound like a wonderful memory. Where would you go if you could choose another place to visit?"

He touched a finger to her lips. "You'll have to land another ball in my cup to get me to answer that."

The game went on until Genna was convinced that both of them were more than a little drunk. She'd learned that Amadio's most hated food was grilled eel, and he professed a weakness for crème brulee. He lifted weights every morning and despised running. She'd shared her own hatred of frozen fish sticks, and her love of chocolate. But as the game had gone on, Amadio had become more competitive. He had grilled her on questions about her grandfather and her life growing up. She wasn't stupid—she knew he was trying to figure out the connection to Camille.

But truthfully, she didn't care. What good would it do? So, she resembled a princess. So what? It wasn't as if she could claim the right to a throne that wasn't hers. If her mother or another relative had indulged in an affair with royalty years ago, it didn't change anything. She was a mistake, an indiscretion that her grandfather had tucked away from the world to protect her and give her a normal life. It was better if the truth never came out.

She couldn't deny that a part of her was afraid the media would find out about her role-playing. At some point, it seemed inevitable. She could only hope that she was safely back in the United States when that happened.

"It's my turn," she told the prince. She was swaying on her feet, but he was smiling at her. He had removed his suit jacket and rolled up his shirt sleeves. His hair was rumpled, and he looked so good, she almost wanted to throw the game to make it last longer.

"One cup left," he reminded her. "You're going to lose."

"I'm pretty good at this game." She tried to aim, but there were two cups instead of one. And they were moving. She closed one eye, trying to figure out which one was the correct cup.

But then, the prince came up behind her, holding her waist. He leaned in to rest his mouth against her throat and said, "I'm going to cheat. I'm distracting you."

"It won't work," she lied. Her skin erupted in shivers when his warm mouth pressed a kiss on her nape.

"Yes, it will."

"That's against the rules," she murmured. "No cheating."

"Cheating happens in life," he said. "Camille cheated on me."

She turned around, and he caught her in his embrace. Though she knew better than to imagine this was real, she was startled by his confession. She slid her fingers into his hair, feeling the sudden rush of desire. "What happened?"

"She had an affair and she's pregnant. It's why she called off our engagement. Not that I would have married her after that."

Genna's hand stilled on his hair. She could only imagine how horrifying that was to Amadio. "I'm so sorry."

"She never wanted me to show affection to her," he admitted. "We both knew it was a political marriage, but I had hoped it could be more."

She understood the trust he'd placed in her by such a revelation. And though he would never admit it, she'd caught a trace of vulnerability in his voice. It made Genna wonder if he'd ever been in love before, but she didn't dare ask that question.

"Does the King of Badenstein know?" she asked instead.

He nodded. "And he also knows it would be very bad publicity if the media finds out."

She rested her hands on his shoulders, feeling a rush of unease. "So that's your leverage against him."

The prince shrugged. "I haven't told anyone yet. Heinrich has the chance to make it right."

She wondered if Amadio would actually reveal Camille's secret. Somehow, she didn't think so, but she focused on the pain it must have caused him. "You didn't deserve to be cheated on."

"Camille always did say I was too coldhearted. I wasn't the sort of man she wanted." His hand drifted up her spine in a caress that belied his words. There was nothing at all cold about this man.

At first, Genna had started this game, intending for him to loosen up and have fun. It *had* been a good time, and she'd enjoyed watching him get competitive.

But now, she was starting to see the prince in a different light. He'd been betrayed and could easily have destroyed Camille for what she'd done. Instead, he'd kept her secret out of the public spotlight.

"You're not cold, Amadio," she said, drawing his face closer. "Not to me." Without thinking of the consequences, she lifted her mouth to his. She could taste the whiskey on his breath, but she didn't care. Right now, she was burning hot, and she desperately wanted his kiss. Just for a moment, before her time ran out.

Amadio kissed her back, winding his hand through her hair. His control seemed to fall apart, and she surrendered to the raw hunger within.

The prince brought her to a nearby bench and sat down, dragging her onto his lap. He cradled her in his arms, even as he took what he wanted. She could feel the ridge of his arousal nestled between her legs, and he felt so good, she couldn't stop her moan.

It was like being tossed in a storm of rapids, the heat eclipsing her. She didn't know when it had happened or why, but she had feelings for this man. It infuriated her that he'd been betrayed, and she understood his frustration. Although she knew there could never be any future with the prince, she had this moment.

He couldn't seem to get enough of her, and his mouth moved down her throat. She inhaled sharply, and he paused before he cupped her breast. Sensations of arousal roared through her, and she let out a shuddering breath.

Though he caressed her, she sensed his silent of question of whether he should stop. She ought to end it now, for this was a dangerous path to tread. It wasn't a real relationship. All her life, she'd been so isolated from the world, feeling so alone. And right now, she wanted to claim a memory for herself, of being seduced by a gorgeous prince.

Slowly, she stood from his lap and unbuttoned her blouse. It was an unspoken invitation, and he helped her slide it from her shoulders until it dropped to the ground. She wore her bra in the moonlight, and he reached behind, kissing her hard as he unfastened the hooks. Any hesitation she might have felt was lost in the storm of his mouth upon hers.

In the darkness, he cupped her bare breasts, and she bit back a gasp at the sensation. He stroked her nipples, and the ache overwhelmed her with a deepening need. It would be too easy to surrender everything to this man.

"Sorry," she whispered. "I've never…" Her words broke off, and she didn't quite know how to finish.

Amadio, however, seemed pleased by her words.

"I'm glad." He continued arousing her breasts, and she felt herself growing wet between her legs. "But I want you to know that I will stop if you want me to." His hands moved to her spine, and he stroked her skin. "Whatever happens is between us."

Her brain warned her that it was definitely going too fast. But if she took a moment to think clearly, she would lose her courage.

Genna closed her eyes, and when he leaned down to kiss her breast, the blood in her veins turned to fire. He suckled against the tip, and it echoed deep inside. She whispered his name, and he turned to the other breast, feasting upon her skin.

It was a moment of intimacy between them, and somehow, she had the instinct that Amadio had not felt this way before either. She reached out to unbutton his shirt, and when it hung open, she rested her hands upon his heart. Right now, she wanted to touch him, for him to know that this wasn't about his title. It was about him.

Amadio continued to kiss her, trailing his mouth up again until he claimed her lips. It was bittersweet, knowing that their time together would soon end. But even so, she helped him remove his shirt, drawing him into her arms until they were skin to skin. She could not deny how badly she wanted him, though she had never been with a man before. He unfastened her trousers, then gently slid his hand below the layers of silk until his palm cupped her intimately.

"Genna," he murmured against her mouth. His fingers slid against her wetness, and he kissed her again. "Are you certain you want this?"

"I don't know what I want," she answered. "All I know is that I don't want you to stop."

"Good." With his thumb, he pressed against her intimately, and she nearly came apart on his lap. The intense pleasure kept her on the edge, unable to breathe or think clearly. Amadio slid one finger inside her, and then he bent to take her breast in his mouth once more.

She was trembling with the onslaught of desire. He was pleasuring her, taking her higher to a place she'd never gone before. But she wanted the experience to be shared, to make him feel everything she was feeling.

She reached to his lap and felt his hard erection beneath her palm. Gently, she touched him through the fabric of his trousers, and he unfastened the waistband, pressing her hand to his hot length. Then he showed her how to hold him, how to stroke his erection in a rhythm. It startled her to realize how much she liked it, how empowering it was to watch his face transform with his own desire.

She rubbed her thumb over the crown of him, and he did the same to her, pressing against the hooded flesh until her body arched to meet his touch. She didn't know if he was planning to make love to her in this garden, but she didn't care anymore. She wanted him desperately, and somehow, it felt right for Amadio to be her first.

"Do you want to go back to the palace?" she whispered.

He kissed her lips and murmured, "No." Instead, he continued touching her, pressing her closer to the edge. She strained against him, her breathing rough and labored. He caressed her intimately while she moved her palm over his thick erection. She didn't know what she was yearning for, but he inserted another finger and kept up his slow, deep strokes, gently rubbing against her hooded flesh with his thumb.

She felt a shimmering pleasure-pain rising within, and she could hardly breathe as he held her. Gently, he kissed her nipple again, his hot tongue swirling until suddenly, the pleasure gripped her in its storm. She broke apart, shattering in his arms as the orgasm claimed her. She had never felt so thoroughly possessed, and she wanted to share more with him. He hadn't experienced the same release, and she wanted him inside her.

But when she reached for him, he stilled her with a hand. Slowly, he withdrew from her, fastening his clothes. It was clear that he wasn't going to take this any further, and a sudden ache of regret took hold.

"We don't have to stop," she whispered.

But instead, he handed her the fallen bra and her blouse. "We do. I won't take you this way—it's not right. You deserve better than this, Genna."

And with that, he left her alone in the garden.

CHAPTER SEVEN

Amadio didn't sleep for the rest of the night. It was more than sexual frustration—it was his own ingrained sense of honor. It had taken every last shred of restraint to push Genna away, for he had no right to claim her virginity. Not when she would return home in a matter of days. He'd let her get too close, and if he hadn't driven her away, it would only hurt her more when he let her go.

He despised himself for walking away like that. It had been cruel, but it was better if she didn't develop feelings for him. Better still if she disliked him. The thought of letting her close was unthinkable. She meant far more to him that she should, and it was better to distance himself before he broke her heart.

Deep inside, he held regrets. She'd given him a glimpse of a different life, of one with a woman who wanted to be with him. He'd never had that before, and it had tempted him far more than he'd imagined. The lighthearted game had been a moment of fun, and he sensed that it would always be like that with Genna—unpredictable and fascinating.

For one moment, he had allowed himself the irrational dream of staying with her or even substituting her for Camille. It was impossible. He could never choose an American for his princess, even if Genna had proven that she had good instincts for public speaking. By letting her go, he was doing the right thing. He would ask Johann to book her a flight home in a few days. That would give him time to make the press announcement about breaking the engagement.

There was no question he had to put his own desires aside and make the difficult decisions for his country. But even as he was writing notes about what they would say to the public, he couldn't stop thinking about her. Genna had such an optimism about life, she brightened the lives of everyone she touched. He was going to miss her, even though he knew he was doing the right thing.

He checked his e-mail and saw a note from the investigator. There was no record of Genna's birth in the United States, nor had he found anything from Badenstein or Lohenberg. It was as if she didn't exist. The only birth certificate he'd found had been a forgery.

Moreover, her grandfather had gone missing. The investigator had tried to meet with him, but no one had seen him in days.

It might mean nothing at all—but Amadio knew better than to dismiss his suspicions. There had to be a connection between Genna and Camille. Whether they were half-sisters, cousins, or somehow related, it made him wonder what other secrets King Heinrich had kept.

Amadio tried to bury himself in work, but it was

virtually impossible to concentrate. Then he turned on the news and saw another story that made him stop short. The reporter spoke of Genna and suggested that she could not possibly be Princess Camille. He gave evidence of the difference in their hairstyle, but even more, he spoke of Camille's former avoidance of any physical affection.

"Her Royal Highness has made no secret of her reluctance to wed Prince Amadio. Why then, would she suddenly change her mind? Moreover, why would she spend a week at the palace in Lohenberg when this was only a political marriage? It's clear now that Prince Amadio hired a lookalike to take her place."

The details were entirely too close to the truth, and Amadio shut off the news. He was furious with the media, but what could he do? Their information was accurate. He didn't think Genna had tipped them off, but Camille might have—especially if she disagreed with his choice to send troops to the borders.

He should have expected this. It had always been in the back of his mind, that the tabloids would somehow guess what had happened. At least they didn't know about Camille's pregnancy. The greater question was what to do now. Should he send Genna home, or would that only make matters worse? He needed to think this through, to decide the best course of action for both of them.

More than that, he didn't want Genna to suffer humiliation. She had come into this situation trying to help him repair a publicity nightmare. She hadn't asked to have her life upended.

Amadio left his room, intending to find her. After a

long search, he discovered her seated at a long oak table, surrounded by mysterious tools he didn't recognize—grinders, polishers, and soldering implements. The moment she saw him, she removed her eye protection and set it aside. There was a slight awkwardness before she finally greeted him. "Hi."

"Good morning." He saw the progress she'd made in resetting the stones and remarked, "The tiara seems to be coming along."

She nodded. "I didn't...sleep well last night, so I started working early. Johann had sent the tools late yesterday, so..." Her voice drifted off, but he had no doubt as to why she'd had trouble sleeping.

"We have a problem," he said. "The media suspects you're not Camille."

She set down the tiara. "I didn't tell them."

"I know you didn't. I think it was Camille who tipped them off. She was angry with me for sending forces to the border."

Genna stood from her bench and faced him. "What do you want to do?"

He paused a moment. "I think we can control the damage best if we move forward with our original plan to hold a press conference and then formally break the betrothal." The storm of that announcement would blot out any sensationalism about her appearance.

She met his gaze, but he didn't miss the emotions she was holding back. "When?" she asked softly.

"Tomorrow afternoon. I'll make the arrangements today."

"And what if they confront us about the deception?" she asked. "Do you really want me there?"

He did, but he understood her point. There would indeed be questions about her and no doubt the reporters would be unmerciful. Yet, he felt it would be a stronger announcement if she stood at his side.

"We won't take questions," he said. "It will merely be an announcement. You won't have to speak."

"And what of the borders?" she asked. "Have you already sent forces there?"

He nodded. "Only for protection."

She grew pensive for a moment. "There is another solution, Amadio. If you'll consider it." He waited, and she reached for his hand, holding it. "Take down all the border barrier and open the roads. You and King Heinrich can redraw the borders equally. The riots are only caused by the restrictions. We're not living in a Cold War era any longer. There's no need for the checkpoints."

Privately, he agreed with her, but Heinrich wasn't about to surrender any territory. The King of Badenstein had his own agenda, and it wasn't so simple.

"I don't trust the king. If I give up half our territory, he won't reciprocate. He'll take everything and leave my people at risk of being hurt. I can't back down."

She squeezed his palm. "So, it's about a lack of trust, not power."

He nodded quietly. "It is." Though he understood that she was only trying to help, he didn't want her to feel obligated. This wasn't her battle to face.

She let out a sigh. "Is there anything I can do to help you?"

He shook his head. "But you will be compensated for your time, don't worry."

"Amadio, it was never about that." Her face grew crestfallen. "I hope you believe me. Last night…even though things got carried away…it had nothing to do with money."

He did. She had never struck him as greedy. Instead, she seemed more intent on doing what was right. He took her hands in his. "I am grateful for your help this week, Genna." He meant the words. Having her at his side had made it more bearable, and a part of him wished it could have lasted.

"I'm going to miss you, Amadio," she murmured.

There weren't any words to describe the feelings she'd inspired in him. Despite everything, he had enjoyed learning about this woman. He would never regret the time they had spent together. And though he would miss her too, he knew he couldn't say it. It wasn't right or fair to lead her on.

When he pulled back, he said, "I will make the arrangements for the press conference."

Genna spent the rest of the morning and afternoon working on the tiara. Her eyes were blurring from exhaustion, but she'd needed the activity to keep her mind off the fact that she was leaving in a few days. Amadio had gone to inspect the border checkpoints, and she was trying to stay away from him. She'd tried to distract herself with another phone call to her grandfather, but he still hadn't answered any of her voicemails. It was probably a good thing she was returning home so she could check on him.

After she set the final pearl into the tiara, she held it in her hands, her mind filled with weariness. She had tried to guard her heart, but in the end, it hadn't mattered. She had feelings for Amadio, an unrequited longing she couldn't deny. Even so, she knew she would never see him again. He wouldn't look back on these days either. And why would he? She'd spent only a few hours alone with him. Yet, during their last time together, she had lowered her boundaries...and he'd refused her.

Was the last kiss one of pity? Or one of farewell? It certainly seemed that way. She stood up from the table and stretched, bringing the tiara over to a small mirror that hung on the wall. Slowly, she lifted it to her hair and studied her appearance.

You're not a princess, and you never will be, her brain warned. In a way, the gift felt like a mockery of the life she'd glimpsed.

And yet, how could she go home and turn her back on everything? It felt like cowardice. No, this wasn't her fight. But neither did she want to simply disappear and take money for her deception.

Genna turned on her phone, planning to find out what the media had said about her and Amadio. She braced herself...but instead of seeing a story about a fake princess, she saw social media photographs about riots at the borders.

And Amadio was there now.

Her fears clenched deep within her, and as she scrolled through the comments, she recognized the rising public anger. Amadio would face danger, possibly violence. And if he were hurt, she'd never forgive herself.

Though she didn't know what she could do to help him, it was far worse to remain at the palace in hiding. She wanted to stand at Amadio's side, for however long that might be. It might help to dispel the media rumors as well.

Genna packed the tiara away and dialed the palace extension for a driver. It was time to do everything she could to protect the man she wasn't supposed to care about.

An hour later, the driver brought her to the border checkpoint. She saw armed soldiers with face masks standing at regular intervals, guarding against the crowd of protesters. There was no denying the fury on the people's faces, and she could see Amadio walking along the edges of the crowd, speaking to them. Genna got out of the car and hurried to his side. She didn't know what to do or what to say, but she wanted to show support. The moment she reached him, his startled look turned to concern.

"You shouldn't be here," he said quietly. "It's not safe."

"It's not safe for you either." She took his hand in hers. "But it will make a stronger statement if we stand together. It will also challenge the media." She met his gaze and lowered her voice. "We're not finished here yet."

He squeezed her hand, his blue eyes piercing in their intensity. Though he didn't want her here, it would be worse if he sent her away. Instead, he brought her over to the edge of the borders.

"This is not the way to bring peace," he said to the protestors. "You need to grant us time. I need Badenstein's support before we can drop the barriers."

"She's not the princess!" a voice shouted. "You're both liars."

Genna was taken aback by the accuser. Amadio was about to speak, but she shook her head. In the Lohenberg language, she stared back at the people. "I want to open the borders as much as you do. And I agree with Prince Amadio. This is not the way to achieve that goal."

In response, one of the protestors threw a rock at her. Amadio tried to deflect it, but it hit her face, even so. He grabbed her arm and pulled her back. "I'm getting you out of here."

The guards closed in on the people, pushing them back, and the crowd scattered. Within moments, the prince had her inside the car. He barked a command for the driver to hurry. "Are you all right?"

Genna nodded, though she'd never expected the crowd to turn on her. She'd done nothing except to speak to them. "I'm fine." She was grateful for his quick action before the crowd could turn more violent.

Amadio pulled out a bottle of water from the car and used it to wet down his handkerchief. He held it out to her. "Put this on your face."

"What about you?" Genna asked. She saw that his hand was bleeding.

"It's nothing I'm not already used to," he replied. His mood had turned more pensive, and only after they were a good distance away did he turn back to her. "Why did you leave the palace? You could have been seriously hurt today."

"So could you," she answered. "You were in the same danger I was. And what happens to Lohenberg if you're hurt and can't rule?"

"My father is still king."

She knew that, but Stefan had done little to help with the situation. "Sometimes it seems as if he has already abdicated his throne."

He leaned back against the seat. "He prefers it this way. He can demand that I make decisions for Lohenberg, and if I make mistakes, he takes no blame for it."

She believed him, for she'd seen for herself the way Stefan liked to manipulate others. But she felt the need to reassure Amadio. "You're doing the best that you can."

He shook his head. "It will never be enough for him." Then he took her hand. "Genna, you shouldn't have come to the border. This situation is growing worse every day."

She squeezed his palm. "Then why did you go?"

"Because they need to know that peace matters to me. I will do whatever it takes to protect my people. And I wanted to try reasoning with them before I have no choice but to send more troops."

She understood that, but the greater problem was gaining King Heinrich's support. Only with troops on both sides could they open up peacefully. She wondered if the leader would be open to a discussion, even without a marriage to join the countries together.

"You never answered my question," he said quietly, letting go of her hand. "Why did you come?"

Her nerves tightened inside with the fear that he wouldn't like what she had to say. She didn't want to make herself vulnerable or admit the truth. And so, she hedged, saying, "I didn't want to be a coward and quietly disappear."

"Being safe isn't being cowardly."

She felt all her fears gather up into a tight knot, so afraid to tell him the truth. She already knew what the outcome would be. Now, even more than before, he would want her to go.

But they had tonight. And if she didn't take a risk, she would never know if she'd missed a chance at love.

"I know we've only known each other this week," she said quietly. "But I care about you, Amadio. I couldn't bring myself to walk away. Not yet."

His expression never changed, but it was as if an invisible wall had risen in place. "Genna, don't say it."

But she ignored him. "I knew what this arrangement was from the start. And I know you want me to go home soon. But before I leave, I wanted you to know that it was real for me. When you kissed me, when you held me. Even when you were barking orders at me." She tried to venture a smile, though it felt as if her insides were breaking.

"Genna," he said quietly. "It can't last. You know that."

"I know," she whispered. "And I know I can never take Camille's place. But…" She paused, so afraid of his answer. "Was any of it real for you? Or was I just a distraction?"

He met her gaze, his eyes filled with regret. "You deserve a better man than me. A better life than this. I was born to royalty, Genna. I know the risks better than anyone. There are threats to my life all the time. I wouldn't wish that on you."

"What if I stayed, but no one knew?" she ventured. "We could meet in secret." While she understood his concerns for her safety, she wanted him to know that this wasn't about his royal identity. It was about being with him, spending time together.

But even as she spoke the words, he was already shaking his head. Her heart ached at his rejection, and now she wished she hadn't spoken at all. Clearly, he didn't feel the same way about her as she did for him. And it hurt so badly.

"Genna, it will only make it more difficult when we part ways," he explained. "I never wanted to hurt you."

It was far too late for that, though she didn't say it. "I don't want your money anymore, Amadio. I never did."

"I will keep the terms of our agreement, including the purchase of the necklace," he said.

It felt as if he were tearing her heart in two. He held only pity for her, and that was the last thing she wanted. "Then it's really over, isn't it?"

His single nod hurt more than she'd ever imagined. She turned to the window, trying to hide her tears. She had laid her soul bare before him, despite the fear that he would not change his mind. And in the end, it hadn't been enough.

The media continued to speculate over Genna, the tabloids proclaiming her as a fake princess. Yet, Amadio knew that her presence at his side today had dispelled some of the rumors. At one time, he would have been humiliated by the stories. But strangely enough, he no longer cared what the media said anymore. All he cared about was protecting her.

When she'd been struck by that rock, he'd been furious. Part of him had wanted to go after the man and hit him, but his first priority had been bringing Genna to safety. And it made him realize that she had become a target, just by being close to him.

God, he'd loathed himself for pushing her away today. She'd been so vulnerable, offering herself. But he didn't want to break her heart. When she'd suggested meeting with him in secret, it only made him feel worse. Their time together was slipping away, and he was well aware that he'd let her get too close. He did care about her, far more than he should. And that meant protecting her from the dangers she didn't even understand.

Outside, the skies had darkened with a thunderstorm brewing. The power was flickering, and he suspected it might get worse.

Genna was leaving him soon, and he had no right to want more time with her. The kindest action was to leave her alone, let her grieve, and let her go. But he couldn't deny that the loss of her would rip a hole inside him. Somehow, she had pulled back the walls between them and had kissed the man, not the prince. He believed her when she'd said she cared about him. No other woman would have risked her life or endangered herself for his sake.

The thunder rumbled again, and then the power went out. The palace generator wasn't strong enough to light all the rooms, so Genna would need candles.

Send someone else to bring them, he warned himself. *Don't go.*

That was the logical course of action. He'd already

broken it off between them. Seeing her now would only rub salt in the wound.

But he couldn't stop thinking about her or her offer to meet in secret. It was tearing him apart. He knew it was wrong, but he couldn't stop himself. He needed to see her again, one last time.

The hallway lights were powered by the generator, but not all the bedrooms had electricity. Amadio found one of the staff members carrying a flashlight and several thick candles. "May I?" he asked the man.

"Of course, Your Highness." The servant offered him a box of matches, and Amadio took them.

"I will ensure that the princess has candles as well." Then he dismissed the man and walked to the opposite wing and up a flight of stairs.

The candles were only an excuse to see her; there was no denying it. But he couldn't stop himself, no matter how much his brain reminded him that it was a bad idea.

A few minutes later, he knocked on Genna's door and waited for her to answer. When she did, he saw that she was wearing a T-shirt and flannel pajama bottoms. Her hair was pulled up into a loose ponytail. Strangely enough, the look was incredibly sexy, for it was real. She was holding her own phone as a flashlight, and her expression grew uncertain.

"Did you need something, Amadio?"

Yes. I need you. But he didn't say it.

"I brought you these," he said, holding out the candles.

"Thank you." She started to take them and then hesitated at the door. There was a heaviness to her indecision, as if she were trying to decide the best course of action. He wanted to come inside her room, and from her nervousness, she knew it. But she held all the power now. If she wanted him to go, she could close the door.

For a single moment, she stared at him in the darkness. Her eyes held longing, but she understood that he couldn't offer her more. There was only tonight.

And then, she opened the door wider and waited.

A thousand warnings resounded in his brain. This wasn't a good idea at all, but he couldn't stop himself from entering her room. He placed one candle on the nightstand beside her bed and struck a match until the wick flared in the darkness. He lit the second candle and brought it to her. "Where do you want this one?"

"On the table," she murmured. But that wasn't why he was here, and she knew it.

Amadio lit the flame and extinguished the match. The room was now bathed in dim light, and she shut off her phone flashlight. He knew he should offer to leave, and yet, he couldn't bring himself to move.

Genna was unlike any other woman he'd met, and yet, she captivated him. Her beauty went deeper, a pure goodness that radiated from her spirit. God help him, he was falling hard for this woman. The kindest thing he could do right now was let her go, for she had no place in his world.

"Amadio?" Her voice was the barest whisper. It was a question he was afraid to answer, an invitation he craved more than breathing air.

He waited, but the space between them was charged. It no longer seemed to matter that they came from different worlds or that he was tied to a country that was falling apart. She stood before him, her lips soft, her eyes luminous. He knew he had to take the first step, to tell her how much she mattered to him.

And so, he took that step and caught her in his arms, kissing her with all his pent-up need. She kissed him back with her own desperation, and he could hardly breathe from wanting her. She had slipped into the lonely places inside him, filling up the emptiness. But he had to be sure that this was what she wanted. There was no going back from this moment.

"Genna," he said, pulling back from her kiss. "Tell me to leave. Because if you don't, I'm going to spend all night touching you." His breathing was labored, his heart racing.

In answer, she drew her hands to his shirt buttons. "I won't let you go, Amadio. Stay with me tonight. Show me what it would have been like if we had a lifetime together."

Her answer ignited his need, and as she unbuttoned his shirt, he interrupted by removing hers. He wanted to feel her, skin to skin. She unfastened her bra, letting it fall to the ground, and he embraced her fully, her softness against his hard body. He pulled the ponytail holder until her hair fell around her shoulders. Moments later, she was naked, and he rid himself of his remaining clothes, drawing her body to his.

He murmured endearments in his native language, worshipping her as he began his quest to kiss every inch of her body. But he needed a bed to do all the wicked things he wanted. He led her back and lifted her into his arms. Then he tossed her onto the mattress until she landed amid the pillows. Genna began to laugh. "Did you really just throw me?"

He kissed her smiling mouth. "I'm not a patient man." Then he imprisoned her wrists, pinning her down as he bent lower. He wanted to heighten her senses, to make her come apart with his touch. She was an innocent, but he loved how she kissed him back with enthusiasm.

His mouth moved to the soft part of her neck, and she gripped his shoulders, inhaling sharply. Her response made him ache for her. There was nothing practiced or false about her, and the honesty only accentuated his own desire.

In many ways, it felt like his first time, for he wanted to give her everything—and yet, as he touched her, it gave him satisfaction. He pushed back the knowledge that they would only have this night together, and he wanted to make the most of whatever hours remained.

He lowered his mouth to her nipple, and she cried out, gripping his hair as he suckled. Her knees relaxed, her legs opening to him, and he slid his hard length against her. There was no denying the slick evidence of her desire, and he reached to touch her intimately. Her folds were like satin, and he stroked her, fully aware of her pleasure as she opened further to him.

"Please," she whispered. "I need you."

He lifted his mouth from her breast. "Not yet."

Genna was trembling with the force of her desire, but this was about more than giving herself to Amadio. She wanted to love him, to take him inside her body and make him see the feelings she held in her heart. Even if she had to leave him, she would claim this night for herself. He would be her first lover, and the memory would have to last for a lifetime.

His fingers slid inside her, and she gasped at the gentle intrusion. Every touch made her skin come alive and the soft rhythmic penetration echoed what was to come. Part of her was afraid, and yet, she didn't want to lose a single moment.

"May I touch you?" she whispered. She wanted to learn his body, just as he was memorizing hers.

In answer, he took her palm and drew it to his erection. She closed her fingers around him, and he exhaled as she caressed his hard shaft. She explored him, learning the lines of his body, and his breathing grew ragged.

"Easy, Genna," he said. "Or I won't last." He took command again, kissing her while he lay atop her, flesh to flesh. She raised her knees, and it drew his length against her wetness. She pressed against him, and he responded by moving his thumb against her intimately. He found the spot that deepened her pleasure, and she moaned, feeling so restless.

"There's something I need to tell you," she said quietly. "I know you don't want me to stay in Lohenberg. And I know we can't...be together. But no matter what happens, I'm glad you'll be my first."

"I do care about you, Genna," he said. "You have to know that."

She did believe him, and she was grateful for this night. It was a farewell, and though it might break her heart, she believed it would be worth it.

He moved his hands over her body, cupping her

breasts before kissing each one. She held his hair as he suckled against her, and he asked, "Do you like this?"

"Yes," she breathed. "Don't stop." She could feel the sensation deep within her, and it made her crave more. He continued to pleasure her with his tongue while he stroked her intimately. She was drowning in his touch, arching her hips against him. Her entire body tensed when his caress softened, and she strained, reaching for her release. A gasp broke forth as he changed the rhythm, rubbing her faster. She was rising higher, her entire body trembling with shivers. Without warning, he pressed her over the edge, and she shattered with a flood of pleasure. He invaded her with his fingers, stretching her as she rode out the wave of the orgasm.

She wanted him so badly, but he commanded, "Wait here." A moment later, he retrieved a condom from his wallet. He tore off the wrapper and rolled it on before he moved to rest on top of her. The heat of his body warmed her, though she was feeling more nervous with him positioned at her entrance. She waited for him to thrust inside, but instead, he merely remained in place. Slowly, he moved a fraction of an inch inside, and she lifted her hips to invite him closer.

He remained patient, slowly invading and withdrawing, barely inside her. It was a wicked temptation, and she wanted so much more. He was awakening the same feelings of need, drawing her back to the edge of release once again. There was a slight pinch of pain, and then he was deeper inside. He paused a moment, murmuring, "Are you all right?"

It did hurt, but she managed a nod. Slowly, he withdrew, sliding back inside. Over and over, he continued making love to her, until the pain faded. The gentle thrusts evoked the tremulous need, and she began meeting him by raising her hips until at last, he was fully sheathed inside. His eyes were closed, his hands pressed against her wrists. She could see him fighting for control, trying to make it good for her again. And it was. She reveled in the feeling of his body inside hers, and she used her inner muscles to squeeze his length. From the furrowed expression on his face, he seemed to like it.

She pressed against him, wrapping her legs around his waist. He was on edge, his body rigid with need. She squeezed him deep inside and when he quickened his thrusts, she met the rhythm, arching to take more of him.

His face was strained, his body rigid as he struggled to maintain control. Genna kissed him hard, pulling him skin to skin until he surrendered.

Over and over, he drove inside, until at last, he erupted with his own release, his breathing shuddering while he penetrated. She reveled in the knowledge that she had made him feel this way, and he collapsed atop her.

Their bodies lay intertwined, sweaty and warm. She kept her arms around him, needing him close. And when he kissed her again, she smiled. "Will you stay with me? Or is our hour over?"

He captured her lips, holding her close. "I'm staying in your bed for the rest of the night. You're not going anywhere."

CHAPTER EIGHT

Amadio had barely slept last night, despite feeling more relaxed than he'd ever remembered. He knew he shouldn't have seduced Genna, nor stolen her innocence. But he'd been caught up in her sweetness, knowing that their time was running out. She had slid into his life like a missing piece, and he'd never known that making love could be so fulfilling. After she'd fallen asleep, he'd stared into the darkness, feeling an overwhelming sense of guilt. She had given herself to him, and he had taken it without any thought of what the future held for her.

She'd said that she cared about him and had offered to stay. While a part of him wanted to believe it, he also knew that Genna had never experienced the challenges of being in the public spotlight. She couldn't possibly know the level of scrutiny she would face.

But she'd already underscored her words with actions. Genna had come to the border with him, to stand by his side against the violence at a threat to her own safety. No one had ever done anything like that before.

And even after his father had tried to force her into the impossible position of addressing a crowd of protestors, she had calmed the storm of public emotion. It made him wonder if he'd been too quick to dismiss the idea that she could learn how to navigate the dangers of a royal life. What if she could?

Last night, she had slept with her body intertwined with his. The warmth of her skin made him want to be selfish, refusing to let her go. But was it right to tear her life apart just because he wanted her to stay?

Amadio slipped out of her room and returned to his office just after dawn. He'd needed the space to decide what to do. He sat down at his desk, and in front of him was an envelope from the private investigator. He'd received it last night but hadn't had time to read through it.

With a letter opener, he slit the top and pulled out a series of photographs and documents. Amadio read through them, one at a time, thumbing through the secrets of Genna's past. Though none of it should have surprised him, it left him with questions about what to do now.

He could bury the truth and let her live the life she'd always known. Give her the gift of freedom. This Pandora's box was one she didn't want to open. He set aside the envelope, wondering if it was still the right thing to let her go. Or did he dare to seize the life that *he* wanted?

For so long, he had lived in the shadow of the throne, believing he had to put his needs last for the sake of the country. But it seemed as if the sacrifice had only tightened his resentment. He had dedicated his life to

Lohenberg, and it felt as if he'd been imprisoned until last night. Genna had awakened him, making him see what was missing. And whether or not it was right, he wanted her to stay.

He checked his email and found a message from the King of Badenstein requesting another meeting. Likely the man was attempting to negotiate better terms. But with this new information about Genna, Amadio had another advantage—and he intended to use it.

This time, the king had chosen a neutral setting. He'd closed off a hotel just over the borders in Badenstein and had suggested that they come up with a revised agreement.

He sent a quick answer, agreeing to the meeting. At least it seemed that King Heinrich was starting to bend. And perhaps they could resolve their differences and find a mutual solution.

After their negotiations ended, Amadio wanted Genna to have a choice. He had never been given that opportunity, and if she wanted to stay, she needed to fully understand the challenges of having a true relationship. He wanted to feel the sense of lightness, the infectious joy she spread to those around her. Her smile lit up her face, and he wanted to see it every day.

A slight thread of concern knotted within his mood. Once she learned the secrets uncovered by the investigator, Genna might believe he was using her. He didn't want her to think that at all, even if her past would cause a stir.

In the meantime, he'd left Genna a note telling her where he was going. He also cancelled the press conference. He believed that Heinrich and he could come to an agreement—especially now. With any luck, Amadio hoped to be back in her arms tonight.

Amadio walked down the stairs and was about to leave, but his father stopped him in the hallway. "Going somewhere?"

"I'm meeting with King Heinrich in a few hours at a hotel."

King Stefan leaned against his cane and sighed. "I think that's a mistake. You've already met with him once before, and he refused your offer."

"There has been a new development."

"Do you mean Camille's pregnancy?" Stefan said softly. Before he could respond, his father added, "Don't look so surprised. I have many sources of information." With a slight smile, he added, "and I do think we should use that as leverage."

He should have guessed that his father would remain two steps ahead. "That was one reason why he wanted to meet. But I have my own reason."

He told his father what he'd discovered about Genna. For a moment, Stefan stared at him, and then a moment later, he began to laugh. "You will cause more harm than good with that information. Still, it's interesting." The king paused a moment and then added, "You're getting too close to her."

He knew that, but he didn't want to give Genna up. He wanted to try for a true relationship, despite the political difficulties. "I know what I'm doing."

"Do you?" His father's expression revealed doubts. "You know she cannot take Camille's place. She doesn't know the slightest thing about Badenstein or even Lohenberg for that matter. If you want to have an affair with her, keep it discreet. But don't delude yourself into thinking there could ever be more."

He met his father's gaze and stared back. "Why?"

The king sighed. "Because Heinrich will never accept any sort of evidence that doesn't suit his purpose. He wanted Camille to obey him, to marry you and join our kingdoms together, old-fashioned though it might be. This meeting is about him regaining control. And as long as his daughter is rebelling against him, he won't come to any agreement."

"Then we'll have to force his hand."

"Be careful, Amadio. Heinrich has already asked me to step in and take back the throne. He's not to be trusted."

He knew his father was right, but he had to try once more. "I agree. But this is one last attempt at negotiation. If he won't meet us halfway, I'll have no choice but to involve the media."

"Just keep your eyes open," his father urged. "Do you want me to come along?"

He shook his head, for it would only undermine his position. "I'll let you know what he says, and we'll decide what's to be done."

It struck him that this was the first time his father had offered advice. He didn't know what had caused Stefan to reach out, but he was grateful for the support. Even if they didn't see eye to eye, it was an important step toward bridging the gap between them.

Genna awoke from Amadio's bed feeling amazing. Last night, she had delighted in his touch, and they had spent hours making love. He had left earlier this morning, but she saw his note on the bed, and he'd promised to return by nightfall. Even better, he'd cancelled the press conference that was supposed to announce the ending of their engagement.

Her heart was full of hope, for she didn't believe that he would make her leave now. Not after the night they'd spent together. Even now, she could smell the scent of his aftershave upon the pillow, and she rested her face against it, remembering the hours in his arms. He had claimed her as his own, over and over. Later that night, she had done the same to him, touching him until he'd shuddered with his own release.

Despite what he'd said earlier, she was convinced that there was a chance for them. And she wasn't about to let him go without a fight. Amadio needed her in his life, whether he realized it or not.

A sudden tightness caught at her chest, for she suspected she would have to remain hidden, as she'd offered. If Camille returned to Badenstein, it could cause trouble with their similar appearances. It would be easier if she got rid of the hair extensions, Genna decided. Or possibly if she styled it differently.

But regardless of what she looked like or what her heritage was, she wanted to be a part of Amadio's life. He needed her, whether he recognized it or not. This wasn't about becoming his princess—it was about finding a way to be together.

An ache caught her heart, for she knew she would have to remain in the shadows. It wasn't the life she'd wanted at all. She was setting herself up to be at the prince's beck and call, available when he needed her. And although there was no denying that he had feelings for her, she was afraid of becoming an afterthought. But what other choice was there?

She'd come to Lohenberg to deliver a necklace and help her grandfather's business. She'd wanted to raise the profile of Seraphina and bring them success. Or perhaps she'd wanted to step out of her isolated life and glimpse a different world. It had been both terrifying and thrilling.

Her mind was spinning with indecision, for she didn't know if she had the courage to risk more, to ask Amadio if she could publicly stand by his side. Only then could they have a true relationship. But unless he agreed to bring her into the royal spotlight, she would be returning to the world of isolation she'd endured before.

He did care about her—otherwise, he would have sent her away and held the press conference. But she didn't know if he could ever love her.

That was what she wanted, she realized. Love. But not merely passion or a fiery affair. She wanted the quiet moments together, sharing their days and putting the other person's needs first. There was such a social imbalance between them that she wondered if it was even possible. Would he ever see her as his equal?

Not unless she could become a princess. And to do that, it meant learning about Amadio's duties and trying to understand them.

Later that morning, she'd gone to his private office. She knew that he kept a table with all the newspaper clippings regarding Badenstein and Lohenberg.

It now seemed important to educate herself on the problems between the two countries. She spent a few hours reading, and when she got bored, she went to look out the window by his desk. It was then that she saw a large manila envelope on a smaller table. It was addressed to Amadio and a photograph was sticking out. At first, she thought it was Camille, but then she realized it was a photo of herself that had been taken while she was in college.

Why would Amadio have this? Had he hired someone to investigate her background? Frowning, she pulled out the picture and the contents of the envelope. Yes, she was being nosy, but if there was a photo of her, she had the right to know what else was in there.

She guessed it was logical that he'd dug into her past, given how he hadn't known her at all when she'd arrived. But it was unnerving to think that he'd done this as if he'd expected to find skeletons in her closet.

There were more photographs of her grandfather's house, a few baby pictures of her, and a copy of a foreign birth certificate. She'd started to set it aside, but then stopped a moment. A chill ran over her when she realized that the report was written in German. And her birth date was different.

Denial rose to her thoughts, along with fear. Why would Grandfather hide something like that from her? Unless there was a connection to the royal family?

It should have been obvious, given her similar appearance to Camille. She'd always suspected Amadio's belief might be true, that she was a bastard daughter or somehow distantly related to the king. It hadn't mattered at the time, for there was no chance she had any claim to the Badenstein throne. But what if they were wrong? She discarded the idea, for it was ridiculous. For a moment, she was numb, trying to make sense of it all.

There was another birth certificate inside the envelope, claiming that she had been born in New York a few weeks later. But a note from the investigator read—*False—not recorded in the state*. Her mother's name, Silke Gutman, was on it, and there was no father named.

She felt almost sick reading over the information, not recognizing the truth from lies. She turned back to the German birth certificate and saw her grandfather's signature on it.

Her head was spinning as she thought of all the fabrications. Grandfather had isolated her from the outside world, keeping her away from technology. At the time, she'd believed he was eccentric and old-fashioned. But now, she realized that he'd been in hiding.

He had always been loving, treating her as his own daughter. And really, he was the only family she'd ever known. She adored him, but now it felt like he'd betrayed her.

What had he done? Had he stolen her from her parents? For what reason? And even more, why had he sent her back?

Surely, Grandfather had known she'd be recognized. Had he been trying to return her to Badenstein in a way that didn't endanger him? Why now, after so many years? No doubt he'd be arrested if anyone ever learned the truth. Or had he been trying to reconcile her with her true family?

Maybe that was why he hadn't answered her calls. On impulse, she dialed him again, but as she'd guessed, he didn't pick up the phone. He'd gone silent ever since she'd arrived in Lohenberg, and she hadn't understood why. Now she suspected his reasons.

Another troubling thought occurred to her. Had Amadio read this report before they'd made love? Was that why he'd changed his mind about cancelling the engagement? Did he intend to use her as a bargaining chip with the King of Badenstein? Her mind was shifting and turning, unable to grasp the truth. She wanted to believe that he'd spent the night in her arms because he cared about her—not because she was a missing princess…if that was, in fact, the truth. But what if he'd come to her because he intended to seduce her into another political arrangement?

Her heart went cold at the thought. She'd treasured their time together as a special stolen night. Amadio had loved her as if any moment could be their last.

She had a few hours before he was supposed to return. There was one person who might have the answers she sought. It was a grave risk, but she needed to know the truth, no matter how dire.

She placed a phone call and asked for a driver to take her to Badenstein.

The car pulled into an empty hotel parking lot, and Amadio spied another black sedan nearby. Though it was a strange place to meet with the king, he understood Heinrich's desire for neutral ground. He could only hope that the monarch had come to his senses and they could discuss what needed to happen with the disputed territory. Amadio planned to withhold his new information about Genna's past until he fully understood the king's intentions.

In the distance, he saw two men getting out of the sedan, but there was no sign of King Heinrich. While they could have been bodyguards, something made him hesitate as they approached. Instinct warned him not to get out of the car.

"Elias, wait," he cautioned. "Something's wrong."

His driver reached over to the glove compartment. But before he could seize a weapon, two shots were fired at the vehicle.

"Go!" Amadio ordered. While the car was bullet-proof, their best defense was to get away.

But instead of driving, Elias froze in place. "I'm sorry, Your Highness. I—I can't."

Amadio barely had time to understand why his driver had betrayed him before the doors were wrenched open. The world seemed to fall into a blur of slow motion. His years of defense training snapped into place, and he lifted his hands in surrender.

He knew better than to make a run for it. Though this was a kidnapping, if he tried to go now, they would shoot him. It was better to wait, for he had no doubt this was King Heinrich's move. Likely the king intended to hold him hostage in exchange for the land. It was a move borne out of desperation.

Then men forced him out of the vehicle, and he kept his hands raised, careful not to make any sudden motions.

One of the men turned to Elias. "Thank you for the delivery." Then he fired one more shot, and the driver crumpled upon the seat.

Amadio closed his eyes, a numbing shock flooding through him. Elias had paid the ultimate price for his betrayal. But the shooting was also a means of asserting command, a warning not to attempt an escape. These men were trained assassins and would not hesitate to shoot him, if Heinrich ordered them to do so.

He followed the men into the hotel. There was no one at the front desk, and they shoved him in the elevator and brought him to a room on the fourth floor. It was a deliberate choice, designed to impede any rescue efforts.

Once inside, he saw two more men waiting. They bound his hands with ropes and forced him into a chair. God, he'd been stupid for not traveling with more security. He'd trusted his driver to guard him, but he should have taken more men. He'd grown complacent over the years, and now he was paying the price.

Just as Elias had.

Amadio's mood turned grim at the thought. It wasn't the first time he'd been threatened, but his stronger worry was Genna. The evidence the private investigator had sent, along with the photocopies, suggested that she was in even greater danger.

He'd left her a note, promising to return tonight, but now, that would never happen. He wondered if she would learn of his captivity or whether she'd think the worst of him. If Genna had any connection to the Badenstein throne—even a secret one—it could endanger her in ways she didn't understand. He'd wanted to confront King Heinrich and learn more about Genna's birthright.

But instead of meeting with the man in a hotel conference room, he'd been taken into custody. Undoubtedly, these men intended to ransom him on King Heinrich's behalf.

None of the four men had bothered to hide their faces. That much was a concern because it meant they didn't care if he could identify them.

"What do you want from me?" he demanded.

They ignored the question, speaking amongst themselves. When Amadio repeated it, one of the men withdrew his gun and came closer. His dark hair was shaved close to his skull, and there was no emotion in his expression. He cocked the weapon. "You speak only when we tell you to speak."

Amadio decided to obey their demands for now and focus on getting out of here. He worked at the ropes on his wrists, remaining silent as the men spoke to one another.

From their appearance and weapons, they appeared highly trained and professional. It was a response he should have expected from the king; clearly, he'd underestimated his opponent. By forcibly removing Amadio as the acting ruler of Lohenberg, his father Stefan would have no choice but to reclaim his throne and negotiate for his son's release.

"How long does King Heinrich intend for me to remain a prisoner?" he asked the men.

The first one returned to his side. A faint smile creased his mouth. "Long enough to stop you from causing trouble." He lifted his weapon again. "And I told you not to speak." With that, he cold-cocked Amadio across the jaw, and pain radiated through him.

He tasted blood, but at least he had the answers he'd sought. This had been retaliation for his demands. And now he had to find a way to escape.

It took hours to reach the palace at Badenstein. Genna had brought the hospital report and other papers with her, hoping the king could give her answers. She knew it was a risk, showing up unannounced. King Heinrich might not agree to see her.

She had chosen to wear a sleek green cocktail dress and an emerald necklace. She'd thought about adding the tiara she'd repaired but had decided that was overkill. Her appearance alone should gain her entrance to the palace. It meant playing the charade a little longer, pretending to be Camille. A week ago, she'd have been terrified. Now, despite her nerves, she believed she would be granted permission to speak with the king.

She didn't want to believe that he was her father. He was a stranger to her, and the thought of being his daughter seemed impossible. The other question was, who was her mother? Was it the queen? Or was it the woman on her false birth certificate? The questions roiled inside her until she hardly knew what to ask first.

The guard waved them through the gate as soon as he saw her. The driver pulled to a stop in front of the palace and came to open the door. He gave the keys to a valet and shadowed her as a guard while she approached the entrance. A servant answered the door and inclined his head as he greeted her. "Your Highness."

You're Camille, she reminded herself. *Act like it.*

"I need to speak with my father," she said. "Where is he now?"

"He's in the library," the servant answered. There was an awkward moment when Genna wondered if he was going to lead her there or whether she would have to figure it out for herself.

"I will let him know that you need to see him." He hurried down the hallway, and Genna followed, quietly dismissing the driver.

The servant turned down the west wing and then knocked on the library door. In a loud voice, he announced, "The Princess Camille is here to see you, Your Majesty." With that, he stepped back and returned to the hallway, a short distance away.

The door opened, and she came face to face with an older man. His hair was gray, and he had a salt and pepper beard. He wasn't particularly tall, but his regal bearing made him seem so. She studied him closely, and for a moment, he did the same to her. From the look in his eyes, he knew she wasn't Camille. But he also knew that there was some connection between them, just as she did.

He opened the door wider and after she entered, he closed it behind her, fully aware of the need for privacy. For a long moment, he continued to stare at her, his gaze passing over her face, as if he couldn't believe what he was seeing. "Who are you?" he asked at last. "We both know you're not my daughter."

"My name is Genna Hamilton," she answered. "And I'm not so sure who I am anymore. I thought you might have the answers." She took a seat, her heart pounding. His eyes were the same color as hers, so it was indeed possible that they could be related. But who was her mother?

The king's expression grew wary. "I suppose every girl wishes to find out she's secretly a princess. But I can assure you, you are not."

Genna withdrew the hospital report and handed it to the king. "Amadio found this. I wanted to ask you what it meant."

He read over the report and immediately dismissed it. "You were born in Germany, so it has no relevance. But I know why you're really here." She had no idea what to say to that, so she remained silent. "You're here to negotiate his release."

She almost asked, *Whose release?* From the smug look on his face, she realized they were talking about two different things. Was he talking about Amadio? She veiled her emotions, wondering if the prince was in danger. Instead, she forced herself to learn more. "Go on."

At that, he expelled a harsh laugh. "Don't try to play games. The prince will remain unharmed, as long as Stefan pulls back the military forces from the border."

Her emotions darted all over the place, from fear to anger to worry. She'd had no idea he had taken Amadio captive. The very idea was horrifying. A thousand questions warred within her, but she willed herself to remain calm. Blurting out demands would get her nowhere. Right now, she had to channel her emotions and gain answers.

She kept her voice utterly neutral. "And you believe that by taking Amadio into custody, you can force his father to obey your will?" If anything, Stefan would consider it an act of war. Despite his physical illness, the king's mind was razor sharp.

King Heinrich gave a nod. "I am done with negotiations. It's time to reclaim what is mine. If that means removing an obstacle, so be it."

He was speaking of Amadio as if he weren't a man. Heinrich's ruthless voice chilled her, for it held nothing but threats. There would be no peace at all, not after such an act of aggression.

"Do you know, I actually came here hoping to find answers," she began. "I wanted to know who my father was. Or something about my past, at the very least. But after this, I'm not so certain I want you to be my father." She tossed the envelope at him. "You're behaving like a bully."

The king appeared amused instead of angry. "I really don't care what you think, Ms. Hamilton."

"Is that my name?" she queried. "I don't know anymore. Even you cannot deny how closely I resemble Camille."

"My daughter Camille was born from IVF," the king said. "We used a surrogate mother." He waved his hand. "There could be any number of explanations why you look the way you do."

"Was Silke the surrogate?" she asked.

"She was. And after she delivered Camille, she left Badenstein."

Her mind spun off and she started to put the pieces together. So far, she could only see one possibility—that she was somehow a twin. Perhaps Silke had taken her.

Genna fell silent for a moment. Though she thought about asking him more questions, it was clear that the king was in denial. He would never accept her because he thought she wanted something from him.

Nothing could be further from the truth. She didn't want to be a princess; she only wanted answers about her past. She wanted to understand who her parents were and learn the truth.

She paused and asked, "Regardless of the circumstances of my birth, don't you want to know what happened?"

"Even if you were my biological daughter—and I don't believe you are—your circumstances would not change. You are not entitled to anything at all."

Her anger grew more heated. "That's not why I'm here. I want to know who my family is. I've been alone and isolated my entire life. If I have a sister, I want to meet her. If you are my father, I would like to know you." She let out a breath. "Or…at least I did until you had Amadio kidnapped." The very thought was appalling. What kind of man would do such a thing?

"Let him go," she insisted. "You've only made the situation worse."

"He's using you," the king added. "Amadio likely thinks to keep our original bargain, claiming you as his bride instead. But I am not recognizing you as my daughter."

"Whether you do or not doesn't change the truth," she said quietly. "My mother could have been carrying twins and kept one." It was the only thing she could imagine. But in the end, the birth had cost Silke her life. "I'd like a paternity test or a DNA test to know for certain. All I want to know is who my parents were. I don't want anything else from you."

The king studied her with an expression of grudging

respect. "I can arrange for a blood test. But in return, you will sign legal documents ensuring that you have no claim to my throne."

"Fair enough. I don't want your throne," she answered. It seemed strange speaking to the man who could be her father, hearing about the life she might have had. She would have been raised as a princess.

There was a pause, and she added, "But I do want you to release Amadio and come to a fair agreement about the land. The longer you hold him captive, the worse this will be."

The king eyed her closely. "I might. If you cooperate and return to the United States."

Her mood dimmed at the realization that her own wishes didn't matter. She had become a complication who didn't belong here. Aside from her fleeting relationship with Prince Amadio, there was no real reason to stay. The answers to her past hardly mattered, for King Heinrich had been clear in his desire not to be her father in name or in action.

She felt the weight of the burden upon her and the terrible choice she had to make. "So, you're saying that you will release him if I leave?"

"And if he calls off his forces," the king added.

She didn't trust the King of Badenstein. This had all the signs of him seizing control of the border lands, and she couldn't allow that. For a moment, she considered the situation, wondering if there was a way to make him see reason. Exposing Camille's pregnancy to the media could possibly be the leverage they needed—but it was a last resort. She didn't want to humiliate the woman who might be her sister. Instead, she tried a different tack.

"If you don't release Amadio, King Stefan will declare war," she reasoned. "You would risk bloodshed for something so petty?" She shook her head. "I see no reason why you don't split the land down the middle. Let the people travel freely and declare it a neutral zone. Everyone wins."

"I'm not about to abandon land that belongs to Badenstein. The people would see it as a weakness if I allow it to be claimed by Lohenberg."

"It wouldn't belong to either country," she insisted. "Set aside your pride and look toward what's best for Badenstein. Amadio will reduce his forces but only if your troops join them to maintain the peace."

He stared at her for a time, his expression inscrutable. Then he said, "And in return you'll leave the country?"

"As long as Amadio is released and unharmed. And only if you uphold your end of the bargain and declare the land a neutral zone." She refused to yield on that point. The thought of leaving hurt her heart, but if that was the price of Amadio's release, she would do it without question.

"I could force you go," he said coolly. "I don't have to negotiate anything."

"And I could cause a great deal of trouble for you with the media," she shot back. "You've already gone too far by having Amadio kidnapped. King Stefan *will* retaliate. And so will I, if you don't meet our terms."

The king stared at her for a time, his expression inscrutable. Then he gave a faint smile. "We shall see."

CHAPTER NINE

Genna waited for her driver at the Badenstein Palace, feeling a sense of unease. She had a bandage on her inner arm where they'd taken blood to do a paternity test. They would know the results within a day or two.

Though she'd agreed to return to the United States, a tingling sense warned her that the king wasn't telling the truth. It was too easy. A man who would go to such lengths—even kidnapping the son of his enemy—was unlikely to keep his word.

More than that, he intended to get rid of his second daughter, so that no one would know Genna had ever existed. And Amadio would believe she'd run away from him.

A cold ache centered inside her. This wasn't the sort of woman she was, hiding or running away. But then again, she hardly knew who she was anymore. Every part of her upbringing had been a lie. Her grandfather had hidden from the world, and for what purpose?

Did he even love her? Or was he using her, too? Why hadn't he returned any of her calls? It hurt to realize that she'd become a political pawn.

Even worse, she wondered if Amadio had been planning to use her, too? With the new information about her birth, had he hoped to switch brides and have the same arrangement as before? It would never work, not if King Heinrich refused to acknowledge her.

Somehow during this week, she had started to want more. She wanted to have a true relationship with Amadio, despite the complications. To do that, she needed to stop behaving like a pawn and start seizing control of her life. Anger ignited within her at the thought of King Heinrich's actions. He'd stepped well over the line by taking Amadio. And the more she thought of it, the more she realized that even if she did leave the country, Heinrich might not keep his word to release the prince.

She got inside the car, ordering the driver to take her back to Lohenberg. Then she scrolled through her phone messages until she found one from Johann Sichermann. Though they might already be aware of Amadio's kidnapping, she texted the Lord Chamberlain, asking him to alert the king. Their first priority was to bring the prince home safely.

Then, she intended to talk with Amadio and find out whether there was any future for them.

Amadio kept a close eye on his captors, waiting for the right moment to attempt an escape. Though he doubted if they would kill him, his head was still swollen from when he'd been struck with the gun.

One of his kidnappers had a radio and spoke rapidly into an earpiece. Then he turned to Amadio. "They are negotiating for your release."

He acted as if he hadn't heard them. His father had known where he was going, and he was certain Stefan had ordered troops to help him escape. It was likely that Lohenberg soldiers were surrounding the area, and if he only waited, they would rescue him.

But he wasn't about to play the victim anymore. Better to risk injury than to go along with these men's plans like a sheep. The element of surprise was all he had.

He'd been loosening the ropes binding his hands all afternoon, and now, he believed he could break free. He just had to choose the right opportunity.

It came within the next hour, when two of the men left to get food, leaving only two guards remaining. Amadio waited until he was certain the first two men were gone. His hands were now completely free of the ropes, though he grasped them in his hands.

"I need water," he said. They hadn't given him anything since he'd been taken captive this morning.

The first man eyed the other, and then he shrugged. He filled a plastic cup in the bathroom sink and brought it closer.

The moment the man lifted it toward Amadio's mouth, he broke free and struck hard. Water splashed them both, but he dodged a blow and threw his captor against a side table. Years of self-defense training came into play, and he fought hard, swinging a wooden chair at the other man's head. He didn't leave until both men were unconscious. But first, he reclaimed his cell phone that had been confiscated.

He dialed for palace security and arranged for a pick-up. As he'd hoped, guards were already on the perimeter, waiting to extract him. All he had to do was reach the parking lot, and they would close in. Amadio slipped into the stairwell and found it empty. He hurried down the stairs and paused at the exit door to ensure no one else was there.

Though he was wary of approaching the parking lot, there was no other choice. He opened the back door of the hotel slightly and took a single step outside.

From behind him, he heard a voice murmur, "Don't move." Then he felt the pressure of a gun against his head. "Put your hands up," the man ordered. "You're not going anywhere."

Amadio froze, wondering if he dared take the risk of escape. It was unlikely that his kidnapper would shoot to kill—but injury was a strong possibility. A thousand thoughts rushed through his mind as he lifted his hands up slowly.

In the distance, he could see his soldiers closing in. They would not hesitate to attack, but the greater danger was the gun pressed to his head. While he knew his attacker hadn't planned to shoot him, if it came down to his life or Amadio's, the threat was there.

The gun pressed against his skull, and he remained frozen in place, wondering if this was the end. But even as the danger surrounded him, he centered himself by thinking of Genna. He would do everything in his power to keep her safe, even if that meant sacrificing his own well-being. He couldn't possibly let her go, no matter what he had to do to make that happen.

She filled his days with endless surprises, and she'd made him laugh. She had awakened a part of him that had been dormant for years. And he wasn't about to lose her.

He spun hard, seizing his attacker's wrists to keep the gun far away. The man tried to ram his knee into Amadio's side, but he twisted to avoid the blow. His arms burned with the force of keeping the gun away, and above him, he could hear the second man approaching down the stairs.

He forced himself to wait, using the opportunity to let his attacker think he'd gained the upper hand.

At the very last second, he tried to wrench control away. The gun twisted, and he poured all his strength into holding the weapon away.

Then the gun fired.

Genna stared at her phone, wondering what would happen now. One of King Heinrich's servants had texted her the details of her morning flight back to New York. The paternity results were still not back yet. Or if they were, Heinrich had said nothing about them.

The more she thought of it, the more rebellious she was feeling. The king wanted her out of the way, discarded so she wouldn't do any damage. And in return, he'd promised Amadio's release.

She didn't know if he would keep his word. Until she saw the prince for herself, she wouldn't consider leaving Lohenberg. She didn't trust the King Heinrich at all, though she'd packed her belongings.

It was nearly midnight, and with every minute that ticked by, her worry grew. She'd tried to text Amadio, but the message was undeliverable. Maybe his phone was dead.

Despite the troops sent by the king, Amadio hadn't returned yet. She didn't know what to think of that, and the growing fears knotted in her stomach. She'd asked Lord Sichermann to alert her the moment they knew Amadio was safe. But there was still no news. She needed a distraction, a way to calm her brain while she waited for his return.

Genna picked up her suitcase and slipped out of her room. Then she walked to Amadio's bedroom at the end of the hallway. The door was unlocked, and she entered and flipped on the light. His bed lay untouched, and there was no sign of him anywhere.

She set her suitcase down beside the bed. For a moment, she studied his room, trying to hold back the worry. It didn't work.

Instead, she lay back on his bed, breathing in the lingering scent of him on the pillow. God, she missed him. Not only the gorgeous prince, but also the man who'd played games with her in the garden. Despite his cool façade, he could ignite her senses with a single touch. With each day at his side, the barriers had melted away. He seemed to value her opinion, and even when they'd argued, she'd felt invigorated by the challenge.

She wanted more time to be with him, to know him better. The thought of King Heinrich's attempts to keep them apart made her even angrier. What right did he have to demand that she return to the United States? Unless he was afraid that she could cause trouble in Badenstein somehow. It made her wonder how much power she truly had.

She was starting to think that there was no reason to obey his demands. Especially when he'd refused to acknowledge the possibility that he was her father. Amadio was still missing, and there was no guarantee he would return.

Genna walked into the bathroom and decided to take a shower. The hot water might help her to forget about the nightmarish day and clear her head. Then she could decide what to do next. Perhaps Camille could help her. She wondered if the woman would be agreeable to joining forces.

Genna turned on the water and stripped off her clothes, stepping into the large shower. The heat eased away her tension, and she rinsed off her hair and her body. She took a moment to wash, but then she thought she heard a noise.

She froze, afraid to hope that it was Amadio. She was about to reach for a towel and shut the water off, but the footsteps drew nearer and then the bathroom door opened. Amadio stood near the doorway, his clothes wrinkled and…was that blood on them?

"Are you all right?" she whispered. "Are you hurt?"

For a moment, he simply stared at her. "It's not my blood."

She shut off the water and grabbed a towel, wrapping it around her. "There shouldn't have been any blood at all. The king said he would release you if I—"

"If you what?" He glanced back at the suitcase in the corner. "If you left me?"

His voice was dangerously quiet, but she nodded. "That was the arrangement he wanted."

He reached for a glass by the sink and filled it with water. He took a long drink, then paused. "Was that what you wanted?"

She could hear the cool distance in his voice. He likely believed it since she'd packed her suitcase.

"No," she admitted. "I agreed to stay for a week. And I don't go back on my promises."

Her hair was dripping wet, her towel barely hanging on, but she went closer to him. When she rested her hands on his shirt, his expression grew heated. Her face flushed, and she reached to touch his cheek in silent invitation. Amadio covered her hand with his own. Then he untied the towel and let it fall to the floor.

He drew her naked body against his own, and she began unbuttoning that awful bloody shirt. She needed to feel his skin against hers, to make him forget the terrible moments of the last few hours.

He kissed her hard, and she welcomed his mouth on hers. He pulled off the rest of his clothes and drew his hands over her body. Then he held her close, his erection pressed against her bare stomach. "I find that I'm in need of a shower myself. Would you join me?"

"Yes." Her words revealed her own desire, and she turned the water on again. He sighed with gratitude as the hot water poured over his skin. She reached for the liquid soap, lathering it between her hands, before she began to wash the blood off him. He took some of his own soap and slid his palms over her shoulders and down to her breasts. He cupped them gently, caressing her nipples. She tried to hold back her own response, but she wanted him desperately.

"What happened? How did you escape?"

"I broke free and called for a driver," he answered. "But just when the car arrived, they tried to take me again at gunpoint."

"Oh God." She hadn't known it was that bad. "I was so worried about you." For a moment, she held him tightly under the shower, so grateful he was all right.

"I'm fine now," he said against her cheek. "I fought them, and the other man was shot. I used my chance to run."

"So this was his blood?" she clarified.

Amadio nodded and pressed his leg between hers. She gasped when he began to move against her.

"You shouldn't have gone to Badenstein," he chided. "It wasn't safe for you there. Heinrich could have had you arrested for trying to impersonate his daughter."

"But I am his daughter, aren't I?" she murmured. "If I weren't, he wouldn't feel so threatened."

"I think you are, yes."

She still wondered whether Amadio wanted her for herself or for her connection to the king. The thought weighed upon her, even as he caressed her bare skin. "I know you had me investigated."

He drew his hands up to her face. "I didn't know anything about you. It was a precaution to understand why you looked so much like Camille."

"I was angry at first," she admitted. But it was more than that. She'd felt as if the life she'd known had been ripped apart. Now she wondered if her mother had stolen her from her rightful home and family.

"I should say I'm sorry, but I'm not," he said quietly. "You deserved to know the truth."

On that point, she agreed with him, but it bothered her deeply, not knowing who she was. And more than that, she didn't know where she stood with the prince. She wanted to believe that what they had was real, but it had all happened so fast.

Amadio turned off the water and reached for a towel to wrap her up. "What did Heinrich say to you?"

"The king...took a paternity test, but on the condition that I would not try to claim Camille's right to the throne. We don't have the results yet."

He took her hand and led her toward the bedroom. His hair was wet, his body sleek from the shower. And his eyes burned into hers with a need that echoed her own.

"I'm going to lay you back on that bed and make love to you for the rest of the night," he said against her lips.

She wanted that more than anything. But before he did, she needed the truth from him. "Amadio," she said, resting her palms against his chest. "If there's no connection to the king or Badenstein, will this still be real between us?"

"How can you doubt it?" he demanded, claiming her mouth. He kissed her hard, his tongue threading with hers while his wicked hands slid over her wet skin. He picked her up and laid her on the bed, covering her body with his own.

"I don't want this to be about politics," she murmured, grasping his hair. "I want you to love me for who I am. Not who I should have been."

He lowered his mouth to her nipple and his tongue swirled over the erect tip. The rush of fierce need filled every pore of her body, and she felt the echo between her legs.

"I want you for exactly who you are." He kissed her cheek, his mouth traveling down to her throat. He cupped her breasts, and he stroked one erect nipple with his thumb. Sensations flooded through her, and she bit back a gasp at his touch. "And I'm glad you didn't leave."

"I didn't believe the king would keep his word. I knew I was causing problems for him, and that's why he wanted me to go."

"I need you to stay with me." He continued kissing her throat, and he lowered his mouth to her breast, enclosing the nipple and suckling gently. She moaned at the shocking warmth of his mouth, welcoming the pleasure as she gripped his hair. When she raised her knees, he entered her in one swift thrust.

Amadio raised her leg over his hip and captured her mouth again. Against her lips, he answered, "I don't know how this will end, Genna. But right now, politics is the last thing on my mind."

He changed their position, pulling her to the edge of the bed. Then he lifted her hips and drove inside deeply. The new position put her entirely at his mercy, and she felt her body go liquid as he began to thrust. She clenched against his invasion, and he began to quicken his tempo. It was like being caressed on the inside, and with every stroke, she grew closer to the edge until her muscles clenched, and thousands of tremors began to take hold.

Her orgasm struck hard, and she shuddered, arching against him as the release poured through her. He kissed her breast again, and she could feel herself losing control as her body took him.

But he needed more—she sensed it.

He rolled her to her stomach and with one swift stroke, he entered her from behind. She let out a cry as the pleasure crashed through her again. She surrendered to him, backing against him as he took her over and over. She felt the driving force of his body, and another savage eruption claimed her. Without warning, the words blurted out from her lips, "I love you."

She closed her eyes, knowing it had been too soon. But her emotions were so raw, so fragile, she couldn't help but say what was in her heart. Amadio gripped her hips, and against her ear, he whispered, "I'm not letting you go, Genna. Whether you're a princess or not."

He plunged into her hard, and she felt the moment he stiffened and poured his release inside her. She felt shaken, utterly undone by him.

And when she realized what had happened—that they had acted recklessly without using contraception—she wondered if he'd done it to keep her here.

CHAPTER TEN

madio made love to her twice more that night, but he was well aware that he'd lost control the first time. It was entirely possible that he could have gotten Genna pregnant without meaning to. But even knowing the risk, he couldn't stop himself from touching her. He'd used protection after that, but the damage was done.

He hadn't been lying when he'd said he didn't know the answer to her questions. Though he wanted to believe that he could be with her, he honestly didn't know what the consequences would be. King Heinrich's refusal to recognize her as his daughter had complicated matters.

But Genna had said she loved him. He couldn't remember the last time anyone had spoken the words, though he supposed his mother might have. The words had wrapped around him in an invisible embrace, warming him with a happiness he was almost afraid to accept. Her love made him hope that anything was possible.

This was the twenty-first century, and he ought to have the choice of choosing any bride he wanted.

The thought of Genna staying with him brought a sense of comfort. He leaned over and pressed a kiss on her shoulder as she slept.

For so long, he'd allowed others to dictate the boundaries of his life. This time, he would do everything in his power to reshape his own destiny.

This morning, he planned to speak with his father about how they would respond to King Heinrich's abduction attempt and the plans for Genna. He'd already decided that he didn't want her to return to the United States. He had a small villa in the countryside overlooking the sea. It might be best to offer her a home there, until he could sort out their relationship.

He got dressed quietly, glancing at her while she slept. No doubt she would be leery of leaving the palace, but after his recent abduction, it would be safer for her here. Before he left, he stood at the doorway, drinking in the sight of Genna. Her blond hair was tousled against the pillow, her palm open upon the sheets. She had awakened him to such immense feelings he'd never known before. This woman meant everything to him. Last night, every barrier between them had come crashing down. He didn't think he could live without her in his life. He'd wanted to give her the words she needed, but he was a man of actions. He preferred to show her instead, by giving her a life she could only dream of.

With reluctance, Amadio left his bedroom and went down to meet with his father. He found the king at breakfast, and the moment Stefan saw him, his father seemed to breathe a sigh of relief. "Johann told me you arrived safely last night."

"Yes. It was very late when I returned," Amadio admitted. It was strange to realize that the king truly seemed glad to see him. For so long, Stefan had been coolly indifferent, but not today. Instead, his father appeared…almost grateful.

"Heinrich will face consequences for his action. But first, there's something else you should see." He passed a folded newspaper to Amadio.

When he unfolded it, Amadio felt as if he'd been punched in the stomach. The headline—Pregnant Princess!—was in bold lettering, and when he skimmed the article, he saw that Camille had returned to Badenstein this morning. He should have foreseen this possibility, but he'd mistakenly believed her when she'd said she planned to stay in Italy until the baby was born. Now, her presence threatened to derail his plans.

"The media thinks the baby is yours," Stefan said. "Especially after your recent appearances with Miss Hamilton."

His mood darkened as he tried to think of a way to handle the rumors. And most of all, how could he shield Genna from the fallout?

Amadio studied the newspaper again. "How did they find out? Did Camille tell them?"

"It seems she hasn't been handling morning sickness well. Possibly a member of her staff talked, or maybe someone who was in Italy with her." His father paused and eyed him. "What do you want to do?"

Amadio took a sip of his coffee. "I need to speak with Genna." He wanted her opinion, for this was a decision they should make together.

"I would keep her out of this," his father cautioned.

"Especially after what Heinrich did to you. He will answer for that, but you don't want Miss Hamilton to fall into the wrong hands. It would have been safer if she'd returned to America."

"No, I won't send her home," Amadio countered. "I intend to protect her. I thought of taking her to the coast for a time. In secret, if need be."

The king shook his head. "She doesn't belong here, Amadio. The media will tear her apart."

But he knew Genna could hold her own. The only problem was her secret birthright. He could only imagine what everyone would say or do once the truth was revealed. Heinrich might reject her, but there was no doubting her resemblance. Regardless of what the king claimed, no one could deny that she had a connection to the royal house of Badenstein.

The only question was how to force his hand.

Genna got dressed, but her mood felt uncertain. Though she suspected Amadio would seek retribution for the kidnapping, she wondered where she fit into his plans. He had been insatiable while loving her last night, and she'd slept late this morning because of it. Perhaps it should have made her happy, but she couldn't help but wonder what would happen next between them.

She ate breakfast alone in the dining room, and when she'd asked a staff member where the prince was, they said he was in a meeting with his father. She realized she was starting to become a puppet once again, waiting for others to tell her what to do. The King of Badenstein didn't want her. The King of Lohenberg didn't want her. And the prince didn't seem to know what to do with her.

Her sense of unrest grew stronger, and she decided to go for a walk to sort out her thoughts. She crossed through the gardens and went to sit at a stone fountain. Water spouted from the mouths of dolphins, and she glimpsed her reflection in the pool. She had so many unanswered questions about her past. And only one man had the answers.

She picked up her cell phone and dialed her grandfather's number again. It rang a few times, but just before she hung up, she heard a familiar voice answer, "Hello, Genna."

"I've been trying to reach you for nearly a week," she said. "I left voice mails. Where have you been all this time?"

"I know." His voice sounded tired. She waited for him to say something, anything at all to answer her question. But his silence worried her.

"Did you know what would happen when you sent me to deliver the necklace?" she asked at last.

"I knew. But you needed to know the truth about who you are."

"Why would you hide something like this from me?" she demanded. "I don't understand how you could lie about who I am."

Why had she been taken away from her biological family? How had her grandfather been involved? He'd never seemed like a kidnapper. But then again, they had lived in upstate New York in a house with no internet. He'd been hiding her all along. It was a silent betrayal that struck her to the core.

"It's complicated," her grandfather said. "All that matters is that you were returned home again. I thought you would meet your sister and…the rest of your family."

So, she was the king's daughter after all. The blood rushed to her face, for a part of her hadn't wanted it to be true. She'd wanted to deny any connection to King Heinrich.

"Your plans didn't work," she said quietly. "The King of Badenstein refuses to accept me as his daughter."

There was a grim silence on the other end of the phone. "I suppose that was to be expected. He never knew about you."

"How could he not know?" Again, her anger rose hotter that her grandfather would do something like this.

"There are things you should know about…my daughter," he said. "Silke was very impulsive, all her life. But she was my only child and I loved her. One day, when you have children of your own, you'll understand how much you would do for your child."

His voice held a heaviness, and he continued. "Everyone knew of the Badenstein queen's inability to have children. She tried everything, but against my wishes, Silke volunteered to be her surrogate."

Her grandfather paused, as if choosing his words carefully. "I didn't want her to, but she went behind my back. The pregnancy wasn't good for her."

"How do you mean?"

"It was nothing physical. But her mood swings grew worse. There were days when she was so happy, followed by days when she wept uncontrollably. We didn't know until much later in her pregnancy that she was carrying twins. Silke begged me not to tell the king and queen, and by then, I could tell that she was unstable." His voice grew quiet, and he added, "She spoke of ending her life because she couldn't keep her babies."

Genna was starting to see what had happened. "Were you able to get help for her?"

"I couldn't. If I'd sent her to counseling—and she confessed that she was going to kill herself and the babies with her—she would have been locked away. Worse, I feared she might face criminal charges if anything happened. And so, I made the decision not to tell the king and queen that there were twins." He paused a moment. "I was not a jeweler when I lived in Badenstein. I was the palace physician."

Her heart started beating faster, but her greatest shock was the realization that every part of his life had been a lie.

"I let the king and queen believe that there was one child," he continued, "and I delivered the babies myself. First Camille…and later, you."

"Didn't the nurses figure it out?" Genna ventured. "Someone must have discovered the truth." She couldn't imagine how their desperate plan could have worked.

"You're right that it was extremely difficult," he admitted. "My wife Eva was the nurse who helped deliver you both."

It seemed so farfetched, Genna admitted her doubts. "I just don't see how you could pull something like this off. It's impossible."

"It should have been," her grandfather agreed. "But you underestimate just how grateful they were to have a baby. The birthing room adjoined another room where the entire family was gathered. I asked them to wait there and told them that Silke was having a C-section. It wasn't safe to have so many people in the room. They agreed without question. And once they had Camille in their arms, it wasn't difficult to close off the doors. I told them Silke needed our medical care for stitches, and that they could have as much time as they wanted with their daughter."

"I warned Silke not to make a sound while she delivered you, or I would have to give you to the king and queen. She obeyed because she wanted you that badly." His voice broke, and he continued. "She was so happy, even though I knew it couldn't last. I knew what we were doing was wrong, but I wanted my daughter to live. If I'd taken you from her, she would have killed herself that night. I have no doubt of it."

"How did you get me out of the palace?" Genna asked.

"Just after you were born, Eva hid you in a large shoulder bag. You were swaddled and sleeping soundly." Her grandfather let out a heavy sigh on the phone. "It shouldn't have worked. We should have been arrested by the palace guards. I've often asked myself how Eva was able to simply walk out to her car with you in that bag. But sometimes people believe what they want to. Princess Camille had her own private nursemaid. Everyone ignored my wife because they only saw a delivery nurse who had assisted with the birth and was going home. I waited a few hours and then I lied and told them I was driving Silke to a local hospital because she needed some additional medical testing.

They never questioned me, and they didn't care that I took my daughter away."

Genna remained silent, still in shock. It was no wonder King Heinrich didn't believe her. It never should have happened. "How did you leave the country?" she asked. "They would have noticed you leaving with a baby."

"You're right," he admitted. "I had booked a private flight to Germany in a small plane that night. At the time, Silke was doing well, and it was only a half-hour flight. We arrived in Frankfurt, and we had another international flight booked a few days later for New York. That was when everything went wrong." His voice trembled with the weight of grief. "We were at our hotel when Silke started to hemorrhage, so I called an ambulance to take her to the hospital. I let everyone believe that you were born in Germany in a hotel room. They gave you a German birth certificate."

The emotion in his voice deepened. "We couldn't save her, no matter how much we fought. Silke made me swear on her last breath that I would keep you and take care of you."

Over the phone, Genna heard that he was crying. Her own heart ached for her grandparents. What they'd done was unspeakably wrong—but she understood that it was done out of love for their daughter. And in the end, they'd lost her anyway.

"Eva and I left Germany a few days later," he admitted. "I told myself that one day, I would do the right thing and give you back."

For a moment, Genna remained silent, trying to absorb all that he had told her. She had to decide whether to accept her true heritage…or deny it. The King of Badenstein might be her biological father, but she was not naïve enough to believe that he would ever accept her. Her grandfather had been the only father she'd ever known. And Eva had died when Genna was a young child, so most of her memories were of him.

"I don't know what to say," she confessed. "I feel as if my entire life was a lie."

"I'm sorry," he agreed. "And so many times, I thought of bringing you back. But it would have broken Eva's heart. She adored you, and you were all she had left of Silke. Even though you weren't her true biological daughter, we thought of you as ours. And we couldn't have loved you any more than we already did."

The emotion welled up in his words, and she felt her own tears rise. What he'd done was wrong, but it was done out of love. And now, she had to make decisions on whether to let the past remain buried…or whether to reveal the truth. If King Heinrich continued to deny her—and if she accepted his decision—no one would ever know what her grandfather had done.

But if she dared to be truthful about her rightful birth, he could spend the rest of his life imprisoned. It might not be worth the risk.

"What do you think I should do now?" she asked. "King Heinrich doesn't believe me."

"He believes you're a threat to Camille's throne," her grandfather said. "You need to reassure him that her position is safe."

"I have no interest in ruling Badenstein. I don't even know the country. And Camille was the firstborn heir, anyway."

"You should probably speak to your sister and tell her the truth about what happened. She might be more of an ally than you know."

Somehow, she doubted that her sister would want anything to do with her. Camille was a stranger, and more likely she would want to be rid of Genna.

"I'm afraid of what will happen to you if I pursue this," she murmured.

Her grandfather admitted, "Genna, once Heinrich learns the truth, he'll try to have me brought back and arrested. It's better if I disappear again."

She understood that, but she couldn't help but wonder if she could arrange a pardon for his past mistakes. If she reached out to Camille, was that possible?

"Thank you for telling me the truth," she said. "I needed to know what happened." Her mind and heart were emotionally drained. She could only imagine how her grandfather felt.

"I know I should have told you sooner," he admitted. "But I wanted to wait until you were ready. And when I saw a chance for that wedding necklace commission, I used every connection I had in New York to get it for you."

She sobered at that, understanding now that it had never been about the necklace or helping her grandfather's business. It was about reconnecting with her past.

"I'll let you know what happens," she said before telling him she loved him and ending the call.

Her greatest challenge lay ahead. Once the paternity results came back, she fully expected King Heinrich would suppress them if he hadn't done so already. He struck her as a dangerous man who would stop at nothing to get what he wanted. Undoubtedly, he would want her removed from the equation.

He was expecting her to be meek and afraid, obeying his every command. Yet, it surprised her to feel such anger and frustration. She had no desire to rule over Badenstein, but it did seem that she'd been robbed of her heritage.

Genna reached into the fountain, sliding her hand through the frigid water. She couldn't deny the trepidation, but she didn't want to leave Amadio. She had fallen in love with him, and after everything they'd endured together, it was time to face the storm and reach for what she wanted.

All she had to do was call the sister she'd never met.

One week later

Genna sat on the edge of the dock, her nerves growing more agitated. Although her sister's tone had been cool and wary over the phone, Camille had agreed to meet her here, at Amadio's summer house near the coast.

Genna had arranged for tea and refreshments at a small table near the water's edge. The morning sun gleamed against the ripples of water, and soon, she saw a figure appear at the top of the stairs leading down to the docks. Though the young woman was slim, not revealing anything of her pregnancy, her complexion appeared sickly and wan. Camille walked alone, and her pace slowed when she grew closer.

"Hi," she greeted the princess quietly. "I'm Genna."

"I'm Camille." Her sister stared at her, not bothering to hide her shock. "I can see why Amadio hired you. It's...a little unnerving to see how much we look alike."

"We're twin sisters," Genna said. "I didn't realize it until my grandfather told me what happened. Even your parents never knew I was born."

Camille let out a slow breath. "It's strange, but I always felt like there was a missing part of me somehow. As if there was supposed to be something more."

Genna gave a nod. "I was raised alone, but it seemed like my life was endlessly spinning in a circle. I just never understood why." She gestured for her sister to sit down. "Do you want something to eat or drink? I...heard about your morning sickness. I thought chamomile tea might help. And there are some digestive biscuits if you want."

Her sister offered a grateful smile. "Thank you."

Genna explained the story her grandfather had revealed, ending with her own question. "What do you want to do now?"

Camille's expression grew guarded. "I don't know the answer. At first, when I met Marcus, I thought he was everything I wanted. He seemed to be an ordinary man who loved me." Her face fell. "Then I learned that he lied about who he was. I can't be with him anymore. And I don't know what to do about my pregnancy. I don't know whether to return home to have the baby or whether I should leave again."

She understood her sister's dilemma. It would be a media nightmare if Camille remained at Badenstein to have the baby. But no doubt Heinrich was pressuring his daughter to return.

"Do you want to be the crown princess?" Genna asked. "If you do, then you should come home and live your life the way you want."

"I don't want to live that life," Camille answered. "It's why I tried to leave. I hated it. My father is…not the easiest person to live with."

At that, Genna expelled a laugh. Wasn't that just the understatement of the year? "He won't even admit that I'm his daughter." But she shrugged. "It doesn't matter to me what he thinks. It doesn't change the truth."

"And what about you?" Camille asked. "Do you want to be a princess?"

"Not at all," she confessed. "The clothes and the crowns might be fun to wear, but it's hard being the center of attention. I don't like public speaking, and I feel as if I never make the right choices." She took a sip of her own tea and then admitted, "But I want to stay with Amadio, even if that means living a different life." Her cheeks warmed, for it almost felt as if she'd stolen her sister's bridegroom.

Camille softened. "He's a good man, even if he always intimidated me."

"He tried to do that to me, too. But I wouldn't let him." Except when he was trying to seduce her. Then, she couldn't deny that there was something incredibly sexy about a gorgeous man trying to dominate her.

Her sister set down her cup. "So, what do we do now? This isn't an ordinary situation."

"I think there's a way we can both have what we want," Genna said. "I have an idea that may work to our advantage. That is, if you're willing."

Her sister drank some of the tea and nibbled at a biscuit. "I'm listening."

After Genna had outlined her plan, Camille winced. "My father will be furious. He'll never forgive me." Then her smile deepened. "Let's do it."

"What are you up to?" Amadio asked. He knew that Genna and Camille had been plotting against King Heinrich, and from the few plans he'd heard, he had no doubt it would cause an uproar. But he admired Genna's decision to take command of her life, and he intended to support her, no matter what she chose to do.

She was struggling with a necklace, and he went to stand behind her, taking it and fastening the clasp. "I'm about to commit treason, I think. It's possible that my father could have me arrested."

"Possible, but not probable."

"I won't be in the family Christmas card photo, that's for certain." She stood up from her dressing table and turned to face him. "Do I look all right?"

He leaned in and kissed her throat. "You always look beautiful, Genna."

"This could go very badly," she warned. "I might have to disappear for a while."

He slid his hands around her waist. "I have a dungeon where I could lock you away. No one would know you're there but me."

That did bring a smile to her lips. "Stop it. That's not funny, Amadio. I'm so nervous."

"You're going to be fine," he promised. "And if anything goes wrong, I'll be there to help you."

"I'm afraid of saying the wrong thing." She stood on tiptoe and kissed him lightly. "But…if you could just be there for me, that's all I need."

He offered his arm. "I will."

She linked her hand with his, and he led her down the stairs. Her fingertips were like ice, and even when they got into the car, he could feel her terror rising. She had never liked speaking in front of crowds, and today was no different.

"Are you certain you want to do this?" he asked. "You don't have to."

She took his hand in hers. In a quiet voice, she murmured, "I want to stay with you. But not in hiding, not tucked away in a house beside the sea. I need to be strong and face what I'm most afraid of."

He needed to reassure her, and he squeezed her palm. "I would never force you into this life if it's not what you want, Genna."

"I can learn what I need to know," she said. Her eyes gleamed with unshed tears. "I won't let you down."

She'd misunderstood him. There was never any question of her being good enough to stand by his side. It was all about her desires, her choices.

"You couldn't let me down," he answered softly. His heart quickened with the rise of his own emotions. He'd never been good at speaking to women. He'd always been a man of action, not words. Time and again, he'd made mistakes, falling hard for women who hadn't wanted him at all. Genna was entirely different. Being with her felt right, and with each passing day, he trusted that she really did love him. Her smile, her arms around him…all of it was more than he'd ever imagined.

And he'd meant what he said. He wasn't going to let her go.

Though he might not have the words she needed, and it was probably too soon, he wanted her to know how much he cared. He was afraid she might not believe him if he gave her words without actions.

"I'm not sure I'm ready to be a princess," she said with a tremulous smile.

His own nerves rose up, and he prepared to take the greatest risk of all. "You don't have to be a princess, Genna. You could simply be my wife."

He reached into his pocket and withdrew a small box. He'd originally planned to ask her to marry him tonight, but she needed to hear it now. When he opened the box, revealing a diamond and aquamarine ring, a tear spilled down her cheek.

"This isn't the best timing, I know. I was going to ask you later," he said. "Perhaps over another game of beer pong that I was going to lose deliberately. Because then, you might say yes."

She held so still, he wondered if he'd made a mistake in asking her so soon. She'd told him that she loved him on the night he'd returned from captivity, but she hadn't said it since then. And when she didn't answer, he wondered if he'd misunderstood her feelings.

"Try it on," he urged. "It belonged to Princess Hannah. You don't have to give an answer yet." He slid the ring on her left hand, and it fit perfectly. But her silence unnerved him. Did she not want to marry him? Would she refuse him, after all this?

She'd said that she wanted to stay with him, and he could give her everything she ever wanted. Was it not enough? The car pulled to a stop, just at the border checkpoint, and the driver got out to open the door.

"Genna?" he prompted.

"I need to think about it," was all she would say as she got out of the car. "Hold on to this for me." She removed the ring and gave it back to him.

Amadio joined her, but his own mood was uneasy. He'd hoped she would say yes and hug him. This silence and her refusal to answer were nothing at all what he'd hoped for.

She and Camille had called the press conference, unbeknownst to King Heinrich. Amadio stood back, surrounded by bodyguards, while Genna approached the podium to begin her speech. She'd worn a sapphire blue dress and a strand of diamonds around her throat, her hair flawlessly styled, but he could read her fear. Dozens of reporters spoke in a low buzz while cameras flashed all around her.

Amadio watched over her as she began her speech. She spoke honestly, about how she wanted peace between the two countries and of the challenges faced by both sides. Although she relied heavily on her notes, her honesty was genuine.

At the end of her speech, reporters began firing questions at her. For a moment, she appeared dazed, but then the questions faded away when Camille got out of her car and walked through the crowd of reporters, surrounded by her own guards. She wore an identical dress, and her hair was styled in the same classic, low chignon.

When Genna saw her sister, she smiled. Camille joined her on the podium and gave her a light hug. Then, to the reporters, she said, "I suppose you're wanting to know more about my sister."

For the next hour, they took turns answering questions. Genna's feet were killing her, but she was grateful to Camille for her help. They had decided that the best way to combat the king's refusal to accept her was to reveal the truth to the media and let the public decide. Even if Heinrich called her a fraud, Camille's acceptance—and pictures of the two of them side by side—made a stronger case.

As they were ending the interview, one of the reporters asked Genna, "Is it true that you are now going to marry Prince Amadio instead?"

Her smile grew forced. She hadn't answered Amadio because he had never once spoken of his feelings. She knew that he cared about her, but the sudden proposal in the car had caught her by surprise. She needed to know his feelings before she made such a decision. A knot formed in her throat and she said, "That's a question for another time. Thank you."

When she glanced back at the car, she saw Amadio watching. His expression had gone cold, like the man she'd first met a week ago. Had he expected her publicly accept his proposal? It was far too soon for that. She didn't want to marry a prince. She wanted to marry a man who loved her. And he'd never said the words.

At the end of the press conference, he surprised her by giving the command to open the gates between the check points. Though they had planned this, for a moment, the crowds gathered at the press conference didn't know what to do. But slowly, there came the sound of applause and cheering. Amadio walked to the podium where he shook Camille's hand and pressed a kiss against Genna's cheek. But his lips felt like ice, and she sensed his anger.

He gave a short speech that she barely heard, about alliances and borders that would be open but remained guarded to protect visitors from both countries. His words were smooth and practiced, revealing his ease at public speaking.

When they were finished, Camille leaned over. "Are you all right?"

"I'll be fine," she whispered. "Thank you for your help."

"Our father is going to murder us for this," Camille smiled. "But he can't deny you anymore. He'll have no choice but to let you take my place while I'm away." Her sister had decided to retreat from the public during the remainder of her pregnancy, giving her time to decide what she wanted. In the meantime, Genna had agreed to take on her public duties.

She answered her sister's smile with one she didn't feel and allowed Amadio to escort her back to the car. Once they were alone, she took off her shoes. He gave orders to the driver, and she had no idea where he was taking her. But it definitely wasn't back to the palace.

All throughout the drive, he didn't speak. His frigid demeanor was back, and with every minute that passed, she felt the coldness emanating from him. She knew he'd wanted her to say yes, but she wasn't ready to make such an important decision until she knew how he felt.

The car stopped near a ruined medieval tower by the sea. It was a strange place to go, and she wondered why he'd brought her here. A macabre part of her wondered if he was planning to throw her into the sea if she refused his engagement.

He took her hand, and she left her shoes in the car, walking barefoot through the sand. She couldn't tolerate the high heels a moment longer. Once they were inside the stone fortress, he confronted her.

"What is it you want from me, Genna?"

His tone held anger, but beneath it was pain. She suddenly realized that he believed she was turning him down. That she didn't want to marry him.

"I want more time," she said. Her words seemed to derail his anger, and she saw visible relief. She took his hands in hers and continued. "I've only just learned that I was born a princess. I don't know how to navigate that life or whether my father will even allow it. And I want to spend more time with you to know you better." She took a breath and added, "I don't want to believe this proposal is because I'm Camille's sister. I want to believe that it's because you care about me…but you've never said the words."

He traced the edge of her face with his thumb, caressing it. "I asked you to marry me because I can't imagine living a life without you." His palms framed her face, and her heart pounded faster. "I can't wake up in the morning without you beside me." He pressed a kiss against her throat, and shivers erupted over her skin.

"When you're with me, I feel alive. You make me feel as if I can be more than the man my father thinks I am." He kissed her lips softly. "And because I'm in love with you."

He took her mouth in a ravenous kiss, and she clung to him, drowning in his touch. Desire burned through her, and she felt him sliding the ring back on her finger.

"You have to marry me," he whispered against her skin. "I can't breathe without you."

"I love you too, Amadio." She closed her eyes, kissing him again and feeling the relief flood through her. She wasn't the princess he needed, and her life had turned upside down from the moment she'd met him. But despite his stubborn nature, she adored this man.

"Let's go home so I can show you how much," he urged.

She smiled in the darkness. "Why did you bring me here to this ruined castle? Were you planning to lock me up if I said no?"

"There *is* a dungeon here," he answered, holding her close. "And I suppose if you want to spend an hour, we could do some interesting things with the chains."

She laughed at that. "Amadio, you are something else."

"Hopefully, I'll become your husband, too," he said, taking her hand in his.

She squeezed it and answered, "I want a long engagement. I need a year to learn how to be your princess. And I want to be sure that this is what you want."

"Three months," he countered. "You're a fast learner."

"Six months," she bargained. "Plus an hour with you each day. Set your royal duties aside and come be with me."

"You can have all the hours of my days," he said, and when he pressed her up against the stone wall, Genna surrendered to the happiness.

Seven months later

The sun shone brightly against the spires of St. Mark's Cathedral. Genna rode in a horse-drawn carriage that seemed straight out of a fairytale. Amadio was already inside the church, as were King Stefan and King Heinrich.

Over the past few months, her father had finally accepted her as his daughter. She was glad that he had set his reservations aside, even if the paternity testing had left no doubt. But he was slowly starting to make an effort to know her. He'd also agreed to walk her down the aisle today.

The driver opened the door and helped her step out from the carriage. Several ladies adjusted her train and veil, and Heinrich stood at the top of the steps, waiting for her. He wore a dark suit with a blue sash denoting his rank and a golden grand collar that ran across his shoulders. When she reached his side, he offered his arm. "You look lovely, Genevieve." He preferred her formal name to Genna, and she didn't bother to correct him.

"Thank you," she answered. Although their relationship was still new, at least he was trying. He had given her a gold and emerald bracelet worn by her mother on her wedding day, and the piece matched the emerald tiara Amadio had given her. She wore the diamond necklace she had brought to him on the first day, and the heavy pendant rested upon her skin above the silk bodice.

"I have a surprise for you," her father said. "Someone else to walk with you down the aisle." He nodded to her opposite side, and Genna was overcome with emotion when she saw her grandfather. He wore a tuxedo, and his gray hair was neatly trimmed.

"I pardoned him," the king added. "He will walk with us...if that's what you want."

In answer, Genna threw her arms around Heinrich and gripped him tightly. "Thank you," she whispered. He could have given her no greater gift. Then she turned to her grandfather and hugged him. She fought back the tears as the two men walked her down the aisle toward the man she loved.

Amadio looked so handsome in his own wedding finery with the royal blue sash, his own golden collar, and the smile as he saw her. Her heart swelled at the sight of the man she loved, and she grew overwhelmed by the joy of this day. Her sister was waiting at the altar as her matron of honor, and in the front row, Genna spied her nephew who had been born only a month earlier. He was held by Camille's new husband.

The wedding ceremony began, and Genna held Amadio's hands in hers. Every day for the past seven months, he had spent time with her. He'd taught her to be a princess, and she had taught him how to relax and have fun. Although he sometimes was overbearing, she was more than his match. He seemed to relish their moments together, even when they'd disagreed, and she could not deny the passion or the love between them.

They spoke their vows, and when he slid the wedding ring on her finger, her smile deepened. "I love you, Amadio."

The warmth and love in his eyes echoed her own. "I love you, too, Princess."

And when he leaned in to kiss her, she couldn't wait to spend all the hours of her life with this man.

If you enjoyed this book and want to be notified when Avery has a new book out, sign up for her newsletter at https://www.averychandler.com/contact.
If you enjoy historical romance, you might enjoy the story of Princess Hannah of Lohenberg in *The Accidental Princess* by Michelle Willingham (Avery's other pen name).

Did you miss Avery's previous book, *Christmas in His Arms*? Read on for an excerpt!

Excerpt from

CHRISTMAS IN HIS ARMS

CHAPTER ONE

The snow struck her in the face while blinding flakes bit into her skin. It was nearly midnight, and Sarah Walsh trudged through the New York City streets in search of a hotel room. She gripped the edges of her jacket, wishing she'd brought a hat or gloves. But there had been no time.

The throbbing pain of her bruised cheek kept her going. *I'm not going back to him. I can't.*

After two years of marriage, she couldn't live in the shadow of fear any longer. Her husband had struck her cheek with his fist, sneering, "If you want to leave, then go. You're an idiot if you think you can get anywhere without me."

Ben didn't believe she would do it. He probably thought she'd come crawling back, broken and subservient.

Not this time. She couldn't.

Her hands were trembling, though it was from more than the cold. It was the bone-deep fear within her that he was right. She had no job, no family in the city, no friends at all—Ben had made sure she stayed isolated. All she had left were the clothes on her back, one credit card, and forty dollars cash in her pocket.

She touched her hand to her aching cheek and tried to push back the fear. *Keep walking. Keep moving forward. Find a hotel. You can figure the rest out later.*

The warm glow of the Harrow Suites illuminated the snow only a block away. She wasn't sure she could afford the hotel, but maybe the rate would be cheaper this late at night. Then again, every room in the city cost hundreds of dollars per night. But she had a credit card, and that was all she needed right now.

Sarah trudged past piles of snow and black trash bags lined along the curb. She heard the familiar sounds of sirens and taxis blaring their horns while men and women crossed the busy streets. Scaffolding set up against a building offered a temporary shelter as she walked past the delicious aroma of a 24-hour coffee shop. What she wouldn't give for a hot, steaming mug right now. Her torment continued when she passed a bakery with glass cases displaying freshly baked muffins and pastries. She'd skipped both lunch and dinner today, and her stomach reminded her that missing the meals had been a very bad idea.

When she reached the revolving glass doors of Harrow Suites, Sarah stepped into the lobby and took a moment to warm herself. She didn't know how bad the swollen mark on her face was, but she might be able to pass it off as rosy cheeks from the cold.

Her hands were still shaking, but she felt better with each step forward. *It's going to be all right,* she told herself as she approached the front desk. *You'll be safe now.*

A woman in a navy blazer with blond hair in a French twist smiled at her with a silent invitation to approach the front desk.

Sarah hesitated, rubbing her hands together to ease the numbness. Another man was leaning against the doorway to the office. He was reading a piece of paper, his expression frowning. His dark brown hair was the color of polished wood, and he wore a charcoal gray suit tailored to his broad shoulders and lean waist. She guessed he was in his mid-thirties, and his face held the look of a man who carried a great deal of responsibility. A manager, she was certain.

When he spared her a fleeting glance, her nerves tightened. He was easily one of the most attractive men she'd ever seen—but then, two years of marriage had taught her that appearances were deceiving. Handsome men held a power of their own, an ability to get whatever they wanted—and that was the last thing she needed in her life right now. Instinctively, she shielded her thoughts, shoving back the raw emotions into an invisible box.

"Can I help you?" the front desk clerk asked. "Do you have a reservation?" Her gaze lingered a moment on Sarah's face, but her smile remained.

"No, but I was hoping you'd have a room available." *As cheap as possible*, she thought to herself. She didn't know how long it would take to find a job or if anyone would hire her.

The clerk's expression turned sympathetic. "I'm so sorry, but we're completely sold out. There's a convention in town, and we don't have any rooms left." She added, "If I knew of another hotel that had a room, I would call them for you. But as far as I know, everything is full."

"I'm sorry to hear it." Sarah managed a nod, as if it were nothing. But inwardly, she felt the rise of tears threatening. She couldn't imagine returning to the streets at this hour in search of a hotel room.

She walked away from the desk but couldn't quite bring herself to go outside. At least, not yet. The blizzard was raging, and she didn't want to leave the warmth of the building.

Sarah walked over to one of the lobby chairs and sank into it. Her gut clenched, and she closed her eyes, trying to think of what to do now.

She'd been so stupid to leave her cell phone behind, but at the time, she was afraid Ben would find a way to track her with it. Now, she wished she had it so she could call other hotels. Instead, she'd have to use the phone at the front desk if they would let her.

Tears burned at her eyes, but she bit her lip hard. *You can't fall apart right now. Keep going.*

"Excuse me," a male voice interrupted. Sarah looked up and saw the manager from the front desk. His gaze fixed upon hers, and he frowned at the sight of her swollen cheek. His eyes were icy blue, and he had a faint dark bristle of beard on his cheeks, as if he'd been too busy to shave.

Her heart pounded at the sight of him, and she tensed. "Yes?" For a moment, she half-expected him to ask her to leave. The lobby was for guests, not for people who had no place to stay. And heaven knew, she looked homeless right about now. Her hair was soaked from the snow and so was her jacket.

Instead, the manager spoke quietly. "If you still need a room, there is one available." His tone held a hint of compassion, and tears blurred her eyes. "Cora didn't know we had a last-minute cancellation."

Relief flooded through her, and Sarah tried to gather her thoughts. She closed her eyes, pushing back the fear. It was going to be all right—at least for tonight. "I'm so glad," she murmured. With a pained smile, she added, "I really didn't want to go back into that storm."

"I would have called a cab for you," he said.

She was glad he hadn't. Right now, she needed to save every penny she had left, and a cab was a luxury she couldn't afford.

"Just check in with Cora, and she'll set you up." Though his demeanor was only professional, she sensed his sympathy. Her throat closed up, and she warned herself, *Don't cry.* Instead, she stood and murmured her thanks again, trying to brave a smile she didn't feel as she approached the front desk.

Sarah gave her credit card to the front desk agent, while she filled out a registration card. After she handed it back, there was a moment's pause.

"I'm sorry, but your credit card was declined," Cora said. "Do you have another method of payment you could use?"

Oh God. She didn't have to ask why the card was rejected. Ben must have called and cancelled it.

For a moment, it felt as if her entire world had spun out of control and back into his circle of command.

Panic gripped her stomach, and she felt the shame rising up. "I'm sorry. I don't have another card," she mumbled. And there wasn't enough cash to cover the room.

Numbly, she stepped back, wondering what to do now. She returned to the lobby chair, and every step reminded her that she'd failed.

Outside, the storm pounded flakes against the glass windows. She needed a few moments to gather her courage. She could try to go to a shelter, but in this weather, it would be hard to find a place. Not to mention, Ben might find her there. She was convinced that he would hire people to look for her.

Hot tears gathered again, but she squeezed her wrists hard to hold back the emotions. She refused to cry. Tears wouldn't do anything to solve her problems.

In her peripheral vision, she saw the manager watching over her. She couldn't stay here much longer. She wasn't a guest and had no right to stay in the lobby. Slowly, she took a deep breath and collected her courage. She didn't have any money for another hotel, but she might be able to slip into the stairwell and hide for the night. It was so late, no one would look for her there. If not here, then in another hotel. And first thing in the morning, she would start looking for a job.

With the decision made, she stood from her chair and turned around…only to find that the manager was standing in front of her.

"I was just leaving," she started to say, but he cut her off.

"No. You're staying here tonight."

Alec Harrow hadn't missed the swollen bruise on the woman's face or the shame in her eyes. He knew all the signs of abuse. When her credit card had been declined, she'd looked beaten down, as if another fist had plowed into her jaw. Someone had hurt her, and she needed sanctuary. He wasn't going to let her go out into the blizzard tonight. If that meant giving up his own suite for the night, so be it. He could always return to his apartment if he decided to set aside the night's work.

As the owner of Harrow Suites, he had forty hotels to manage along the east coast and another hundred hotels in Europe. One room was reserved for him in every hotel, and he made a habit of dropping in without notifying the staff. It was the best way to ensure that the hotels were running smoothly, and he prided himself on the chain he had built.

Alec studied the young woman discreetly for a moment. She was slender with shoulder length honey blond hair and a heart-shaped face. Her green eyes held such pain, he wondered how any man could try to hurt a woman. A large diamond rested on her left hand, and he suspected her husband had caused the blow. She wore jeans and an oversized sweatshirt that hid her figure. Her jacket was unzipped, but it was only a windbreaker—not nearly enough to push back the cold wintry air.

But more than that, he saw the stubborn pride in her face as she stood up to face him. "I'll be all right."

The woman was going to walk out of the hotel and into a blizzard, wearing that pitiful excuse for a coat. He could tell that she'd left with the clothes on her back and hardly anything to call her own. She wouldn't accept his help, and if he didn't stop her, she would leave.

He couldn't tell her that he was giving up his own room for her use, so instead, he thought up a lie.

"It was a mistake. The credit card went through the second time when I told Cora to try it again. It must have been a system malfunction."

The look of relief on her face was stunning. "Really?" She closed her eyes a moment, and then smiled. "I'm so glad."

He didn't return the smile. Seeing her circumstances only brought back all the memories he'd tried to bury over the years. He had a thousand unanswered questions about this woman, but he knew better than to ask.

Don't get involved, he warned himself. *It's not your battle to fight.* He knew that, and yet, he couldn't stand by and let this woman go out in a blizzard on a night like this.

He escorted her back to the front desk and said, "Cora will get you the key cards, but you'll need to wait until the room is made up. I'll call Housekeeping." Jasmine lived down the street, and he could offer her overtime pay to come in and clean the room.

Alec excused himself to make the call while the woman signed the registration card. He stood at the doorway with the phone in his hand, though he hadn't even dialed the number. Eavesdropping was much easier that way.

Cora put two plastic keycards in an envelope and said, "I'll hold on to these for now until your room is ready. If you have a cell phone number, I'll text you when the room is ready."

"I don't...have my phone with me," the woman said. "I'll just wait in the lobby if that's all right."

205

"Of course," Cora said brightly. "There's coffee at the station over there. Help yourself."

Alec watched as the young woman walked back to the lobby chair. The pieces were starting to come together. She had no cell phone. One credit card that had been cancelled. Likely very little cash, and he didn't know if she'd eaten a meal tonight. After she left the desk, he made the call to Jasmine and then a second call to room service for a tray of food.

"Mr. Harrow?" Cora asked in a low voice. "Are you sure about this?"

"That bruise didn't come from a fall," he muttered. "And yes. It's only for one night." He hadn't planned on sleeping much anyway. This property wasn't making enough of a profit, and he needed to spend time with the accounts and unravel where the problems were. He could work in the office for a few hours and return home once it was finished.

Cora had a worried look on her face, but she nodded. "You're a good man, Mr. Harrow."

"Don't tell anyone." The business world wasn't kind to the softhearted. He'd built Harrow Suites from a small boutique hotel in the city, taking endless risks until he'd created a worldwide hotel chain. It was a fragile empire, but when it came to expansion, most of his rivals knew better than to underestimate him.

With that, Alec closed the office door, trying not to think of the woman in the lobby. He brought up a few of the spreadsheets he'd been working on, but he couldn't concentrate. The numbers blurred together, and after half an hour, he gave up. A knock sounded at the door, and when he called out, "Come in," he saw that the room service tray had arrived. He'd been careful to choose an assortment of appetizers, cookies, and soft drinks instead of a full meal.

"Thank you." He signed for the charge and added a generous tip before he picked up the tray and walked into the lobby.

The woman was sitting in a large chair with her knees tucked beneath her while she stared out at the falling snow. It took her a moment before she noticed him standing there with the tray.

"You missed our complimentary appetizer hour," he said. "We usually offer our guests drinks and snacks in the evening. I thought you might be hungry."

She glanced at the tray as if she wanted to refuse, but her eyes lingered on a brownie. Her mouth pursed as if she were trying to keep from reacting to the food. When she hesitated, he asked, "Would you rather have a soft drink or coffee?"

The mention of a hot drink brought a warmth to her eyes. "Coffee would be great." She drew her knees down and stared at the tray.

"Cream and sugar?"

She nodded but didn't speak. Alec walked toward the coffee station but caught a glimpse of her reaching for the brownie. She ate the entire thing in two bites, and the hard knot in his gut drew tighter. Then she reached for a cookie, making him wonder how long it had been since she'd eaten.

He poured the coffee and brought over a second cup filled with flavored creamer cups and sweetener packets. She stopped eating the cookie and her face turned sheepish. "My grandma always said to start with dessert first. That way you always have room."

Alec passed her the coffee and she held it a moment, warming her hands. Then she added four creamer pods and three packets of sugar. For a moment, she reminded him of a little girl, doctoring up her coffee.

"Do you want a cookie before I eat them all?" she offered. With a wry smile, she said, "I probably will."

Alec shook his head. "I've already eaten." He hadn't, really, but he wasn't about to take her cookies. Not when she was clearly so hungry. "I'll leave you to them."

"Thank you, Mr…?" She let the question trail away, but he wasn't about to give his last name. Not when she could connect his identity to the hotel chain.

"You can call me Alec. And it was my pleasure."

"I'm Sarah." She didn't offer her last name, and he didn't ask. It was better for them to remain strangers.

He intended to leave but couldn't quite bring himself to go. At least, not yet. "Is there anything else you need?"

"Not unless a job is something else you have on that tray," she remarked before she shook her head. "I'm just kidding. Thank you for your help. I really do appreciate it." This time, her mouth curved in a genuine smile. It lit up her face with a softness and beauty that caught him off guard. Though her blond hair was still wet from the snow and a tangled mess, he found her fascinating.

He turned away and saw Cora raising her hand to catch his attention. Then she pointed toward Sarah and held up the key card packet.

"Your room is ready," he told her. "You can finish eating first if you like. Or take the tray with you." Though he already knew the answer, he asked, "Do you have any luggage you need brought up to the room?"

She shook her head. "No, I don't have anything." His gaze fixed on the bruise on her face, and she blushed at his stare.

He understood her need to keep that boundary intact. "I'll send up some of our complimentary toiletries. Enjoy your stay."

Her room was at the end of a long hallway. When Sarah put the keycard inside the slot and opened the door, she was startled to realize that Alec had given her the largest suite in the hotel. The lights were already on, and the carpet had just been vacuumed. The room smelled clean, and it had a large living room and a desk that faced a floor-to-ceiling glass window overlooking the city. A king-sized bed stood at the opposite end of the room, and there was a small bar with a silver tray and an ice bucket upon it.

There was a familiar scent within the room, like a man's aftershave. It took her a moment to realize what it was. Or, in this case, *who* it was.

Alec had given her his own room. She couldn't say just how she knew, but she was sure of it. Though it was foolish, she returned to the door and deadbolted it before flipping the latch over. He didn't seem like the sort of man to lure an unsuspecting woman into his room, but she was taking no chances.

Outside, the snow raged against the windows, piling up on the street. Lines of cars were stopped in traffic, despite the late hour. Sarah picked up a blanket from the edge of the bed and wrapped herself inside it. She felt the familiar rise of anxiety as she wondered what she would do tomorrow. Somehow, she had to find work. But a fast-food job wouldn't pay enough for a hotel room.

She had a degree in interior design that she'd never used. But what good was that? It would take time to earn the money she needed. No, the higher priority was finding a place to stay that was within her budget. A hotel wasn't a good solution, since Ben could cancel the credit card at any time—not to mention, he might not pay the bill.

A twist of nausea caught her stomach, and she gripped the edges of the blanket, feeling lost. But instead of pitying herself, she tried to look at the positive moments of the day. She had a warm bed to sleep in, and Alec had brought her food.

Just thinking of him brought a flush of embarrassment. It had been so long since a man had been kind to her instead of ordering her around. Ben had controlled every moment of her day, from the time she woke up, to what she wore, to the way she lived her life. Everything had revolved around him.

She'd been so stupid to fall for her husband's romantic gestures. At the time, she had been flattered by the two dozen roses or the gold watch he'd given her after only one month of dating. What woman didn't want to fall in love with a rich man who seemed to adore her?

She had married him only six months after she'd met him, star-struck by the man who had showered her with affection. But Ben didn't know the meaning of love. Once she'd moved in with him, the imprisonment had begun.

"You won't need to get a job, Sarah," he'd said. "I've already cancelled your interviews."

She'd been shocked that he would do such a thing, but his eyes had softened. "I'm going to take care of you. I make enough money, so you don't have to work. I've arranged for everything you need."

He'd opened the closet to reveal dozens of designer labels, matching shoes, and handbags. All were arranged by color, the garment hangers facing the same direction. At the time, she'd been thrilled by the gift, believing that he was the most generous husband. But it was only the beginning.

"Your stylist has made a list of what you are to wear each day. You will be expected to look your best at all times, especially when we entertain guests at home. You will never leave without your make-up on or your hair done." He stepped back, his face somber. "I know you aren't accustomed to attending formal events, and that isn't something I expect or want from you. In fact, I want to keep our marriage a low profile. I value my privacy, and I want to protect you. The media isn't kind."

It was as if he'd wanted to hide her from the world. Sarah had argued that she was perfectly happy to attend parties with him, only to realize that he had no intention of taking her out in public. He had been grooming her for the role of a subservient wife who stayed at home to meet his every need.

Ben had donated all her old clothing, but she'd managed to save one sweatshirt and one pair of jeans. When she'd worn the sweatshirt on her escape to this hotel, it had felt like she was holding on to a precious memory, as if her mother were watching over her. The sweatshirt was one that Rosalie had owned, years ago. It was the last memory Sarah had of her before her mother had died of cancer.

She didn't even realize she was crying until the phone rang, interrupting her thoughts. It was late, nearly one-thirty, and she wondered if it was the front desk or Alec. When she picked up the phone, she answered, "Hello?"

"I'm glad you found a place to stay, Sarah."

Bile rose up in her throat, and the blood seemed to freeze in her veins. She nearly hung up on her husband, but managed to ask, "H-how did you find me, Ben?"

"The credit card charge. It wasn't difficult." His voice had that smug quality that she loathed. "I asked them to notify me of the first charge after I froze the account. I'm surprised you had enough cash to cover the room."

She said nothing, trying to gather command of her emotions. So, her suspicions had been right. This was Alec's room, and he'd allowed her to stay, free of charge.

"I will send a car to pick you up in the morning," he said. "And you will not attempt to run away again."

This time, she did hang up. And when the phone rang a moment later, she let it go to voice mail. The last thing she wanted was to hear her husband's commands. Instead, Sarah went into the bathroom to run the shower. She turned on the hot water and rested her hands against the sink as the mirror fogged up.

Anger and frustration raged within her. Ben expected her to return to the prison she'd endured within their marriage—after he punished her, that is. She could only imagine what he would do to her for running away.

When she wiped the humidity from the mirror, she studied her swollen cheek, which was already starting to bruise. He would only hurt her again if she went back. Next time, he might break her ribs or worse. She couldn't do it. Not again.

You're going to be strong now. You have to be.

Did you enjoy the excerpt?
"Christmas in His Arms" is available in print at Amazon and on the author's website:
www.averychandler.com

It can also be downloaded from all e-book retailers.

Avery Chandler lives in Virginia with her children, her dog, and her two crazy cats. When she's not rescuing her youngest cat from climbing the walls, she enjoys writing more romances. Avery's favorite hobbies include baking desserts, completing jigsaw puzzles, playing the piano, and traveling around the world whenever possible. Visit her website at: www.averychandler.com. Avery also writes historical romance under the pen name Michelle Willingham.